"Am I missing something here?" Mateo frowned and Alice didn't say anything. She just met his frowning gaze steadily.

"I haven't come here to try and reconnect with you, Mateo. Believe it or not, I'm not the type of person who finds out someone's worth and then decides that they're worth cultivating."

"I don't understand."

"I've come here..."

"You maybe want me to donate something to your school?"

She laughed. It was too absurd. "Well, St. Christopher's could certainly do with an injection of cash, but I haven't come here to ask for funding. I came here to tell you...to tell you..."

"I'm all ears, Alice. Take me somewhere new and challenging that explains your presence here..."

He sat forward, shot her a darkly wolfish smile and rested his arms on the desk, and Alice said what she had come to say in a rush.

"I'm pregnant, Mateo. I came here to tell you that I'm having a baby!"

Cathy Williams can remember reading Harlequin books as a teenager, and now that she is writing them, she remains an avid fan. For her, there is nothing like creating romantic stories and engaging plots, and each and every book is a new adventure. Cathy lives in London, and her three daughters—Charlotte, Olivia and Emma—have always been, and continue to be, the greatest inspirations in her life.

Books by Cathy Williams

Harlequin Presents

Consequences of Their Wedding Charade
Hired by the Forbidden Italian
Bound by a Nine-Month Confession
A Week with the Forbidden Greek
The Housekeeper's Invitation to Italy
The Italian's Innocent Cinderella
Unveiled as the Italian's Bride
Bound by Her Baby Revelation
Emergency Engagement

Secrets of Billionaires' Secretaries

A Wedding Negotiation with Her Boss
Royally Promoted

Visit the Author Profile page
at Harlequin.com for more titles.

SNOWBOUND THEN PREGNANT

CATHY WILLIAMS

PRESENTS

Harlequin® PRESENTS™

ISBN-13: 978-1-335-93942-5

Snowbound Then Pregnant

Copyright © 2024 by Cathy Williams

Recycling programs for this product may not exist in your area.

For questions and comments about the quality of this book, please contact us at CustomerService@Harlequin.com.

TM and ® are trademarks of Harlequin Enterprises ULC.

Harlequin Enterprises ULC
22 Adelaide St. West, 41st Floor
Toronto, Ontario M5H 4E3, Canada
www.Harlequin.com

Printed in Lithuania

MIX
Paper | Supporting responsible forestry
FSC® C021394

SNOWBOUND THEN PREGNANT

CHAPTER ONE

ALICE WAS BEGINNING to wonder whether this was going to be the day she finally met The Big Guy Up There— the very one her dad preached about in his sermons every Sunday.

The cold on her face stung, and even through the layers of protective ski-gear she could feel the whip of the freezing blizzard doing its best to turn her into an ice sculpture. She could barely see in front of her.

She had no idea how much time had gone by since she'd left the chalet where she and her three friends were staying: an hour? Three hours? Fifteen minutes? A year and a half? She'd forgotten her fitness watch in her hurry to leave and her phone was embedded so deeply into one of the pockets of her under-layers that to stop and unearth it would risk instant hypothermia.

Of course, she should never have ventured out, but hindsight was a wonderful thing, and at the time she'd just *had* to get some air: it had felt like the most straight-forward decision in the world.

Bea had been proudly showing off her engagement ring, a surprise revelation she had been keeping up her sleeve for the right 'Ta da!' moment. Out had come the

champagne; the popping of the cork had been punctu-
ated by lots of squeals of delight, a flood of eager questions and excited talk about bridesmaids' dresses. Just
like that, Alice had felt the world closing in on her.

She'd sat there, smiling and twirling the champagne
flute between her fingers, thinking back to her own broken engagement eight months ago. Everything had been
ticked on her 'ideal for permanent partner' checklist...
and yet, Simon had just not been right, had just not been
enough, had just not been what she'd wanted after all.
Everything about him had made sense yet, in the end,
none of it had made any sense at all.

So what if she'd been the one to screw up the cour-
age to do the breaking off? She still had scars left from
the whole sorry business, and those scars had suddenly flared up, raw and painful, as she'd listened to
her friends blown away by the thrill of an upcoming
wedding.

She'd just had to escape, and hadn't been able to stay
put, pretending that she wasn't tearing up inside, so
she'd stood up and announced that she needed to have
a breather. The fact that they had all instantly seen her
upset and rushed to apologise for being thoughtless had
only made the whole situation worse.

So here she was now, no longer skiing but moving
clumsily at a snail's pace, because she couldn't see what
was in front of her with thoughts of hypothermia and
meeting her maker uppermost in her mind.

She was scared witless.

An hour, three hours, a *lifetime* ago there had been
fellow skiers on the slopes, but now the vast stretch of

white was empty. She had skied away from the buzz of people, wanting the peace of solitude on the more dangerous pistes, and when the blizzard had roared in as sudden as a clap of thunder she had been alone.

Now she was desperately hunting for any signpost or landmark to orient her and show her a way back to civilisation, but the driving force of the snow was making it impossible. Panic was rising, but Alice knew that was something she had to block out, because panic in a situation like this equalled certain death. She was too experienced to go down that road.

A blizzard was the most dangerous condition on a mountain: people couldn't see and the snow and moisture in the air made them lose heat very quickly. Those were basic 'fun facts' that had been drummed into all of her class as school kids over a decade ago before they'd gone on their first ever school holiday to Mont Blanc. They were also the very same fun facts she had drummed into her newbies when she had done six months of ski instruction during her gap year, on the very same slopes, less than four years ago.

Basically, no one in their right mind wanted to be out on a mountain in a blizzard—yet here she was. She stopped, tilted up her ski goggles and surveyed a scene of endless, driving snow, blowing this way and that as though driven by a giant, high-speed fan somewhere up in the sky. She was gripped by a momentary wave of sickening fear because the wilderness of white was so menacing, so alien. She could have been on another planet.

Keep making your way down and you'll get to safety—law of averages and basic rule of thumb.

But, when it came to lessons learnt from this whole adventure, sudden attacks of emotion were only *ever* going to be given airtime in the comfort and safety of her living room, preferably with a tub of ice-cream to hand.

She breathed in deeply and propelled her way onward with the speed of someone with weights strapped to their ankles swimming in treacle.

She had no idea how long it was before, at last, she saw *something*: a light, just a flicker penetrating the wall of snow. It was barely visible, and it might have just been an illusion, her fevered brain playing tricks on her, but at this point Alice didn't really care. What were her choices? Illusion or no illusion, she was just going to have to go in that direction. There was no room for hesitation or fear because she was flat out of options.

Mateo was in the middle of preparing his evening meal when he heard something: the vaguest hint of something which was barely audible over the jazz music playing softly in the background. The angry howls of the blizzard outside had been reduced to murmurs because his chalet was triple-glazed to within an inch of its life. He stilled, turned off the music and tilted his head, every one of his senses on full alert.

Here on this gloriously isolated and tucked-away side of Mont Blanc, the chances of skiers dropping by for a cup of coffee were non-existent. This part of the mountain, with its treacherous slopes, was suitable only for experts and was usually so empty that it could have been his own private playground.

It had been a definite selling point when he had bought the place several years ago. He had no problem with the jolly troops of revellers who had fun in the many chic resorts on the mountain…just as long as they didn't come near him.

So he was banking on whatever he'd heard producing the thump against his front door being the whipping snowstorm outside. Some idiot lost in this treacherous blizzard would test his patience to the limit and Mateo really didn't want his patience being tested to the limit right now. Any other time, maybe, but here, now—no.

He was here for a week, seven snatched days. This was his one and only pure time-out from the gruelling business of running his network of companies and living life in the fast lane. He'd been here for two days and the last thing he wanted was any of the remaining five to be interrupted by a risk-taking fool.

Here, and only here, did Mateo come close to reconnecting with a past he had long since left behind, a past that contained none of the often tiresome trappings that went with the sort of wealth he had accumulated. It was important to him that he never forget his beginnings. He had grown up in this part of the world—not on this side of the mountain but in a village close to one of the cheaper resorts—in a small house with struggling young parents, both of whom had worked at a low-end resort for minimum pay. In the high season they'd depended on tips to top up the coffers and, in the low season, they'd taken summer work wherever they could find it. They hadn't been proud.

Lord knew, things would have remained that way for ever had his mother not died when Mateo was twelve. After that, his memories were a blur of sadness, confusion, grief and then, as one year had turned into two and then three, the dawning realisation that he was growing up on his own because his still-young father just hadn't been able to cope without his wife as his rock, by his side.

Mateo had watched from the side lines as his dad had managed to hold down a job at the resort for a couple more seasons. It had been a struggle, because drinking and drugs had begun to make twin inroads into his ability to work, and then eventually his ability to do anything at all—including his ability to look after himself, never mind his precociously bright teenaged son who had been left on his own to cope.

Mateo had quit school at sixteen to begin the process of earning money because his father hadn't been able to keep his head above water. He'd had to balance earning money to pay the bills, because no one else had been around to do it, with studying to make sure he never ended up poor and dependent on the goodwill of others to pick up the slack. Keeping his education on track outside of the school system had became the ultimate goal. He'd known he had a good brain—better than good. He hadn't intended to waste it, or to flush his future down the drain side by side with his father.

He'd begun working at a local boxing gym. For fun, he'd boxed as an amateur and had challenged himself to win every match he'd played but mostly he'd fallen into a routine of working by day and studying by night. He'd been smart—too smart for the online courses, too smart for the problems posed in exams, but smart enough to see where his talents lay and to take advantage of his gift for maths by entering the complex world of coding.

And from there to where he was now. From a seventeen-year-old kid developing a website for his coach, to the eighteen-year-old being paid to design for someone else, and then wanting more than just working for other people; wanting more than just standing still.

He'd saved and become a hunter, the guy who knew just where to find the next big start-up. The guy who turned everything he touched to gold. By his late twenties, he'd been invincible. Winning had become his goal and winning had got him the sort of wealth most people could only dream of.

That said, Mateo knew that it was easy to forget the road that had taken a person from rags to riches, and to forget that road was to risk forgetting lessons learnt along the way. Rags to riches could end up as rags again in the blink of an eye. All that was needed was a little too much laziness and a little too much complacency.

Being here on the mountain was a reminder. His father no longer lived here. Mateo himself lived in London, with places in New York, Hong Kong and Dubai, but this quiet corner on the slopes was a sliver of a distant past.

The merest hint that some clown might now invade his sanctuary filled Mateo with grim rage. Quite still, and ear cocked, he heard the bang on the door with a sinking heart, well aware that he could hardly turn away whatever dope might be shivering outside. Dope or *dopes*: lads who'd decided to play fast and loose with their own lives, safe in the misguided juvenile delusion that someone would magically materialise to save their sorry skins.

He switched off the stove and padded barefoot to open the door.

Alice was about to bang on the door for the third time when it was pulled open without warning and she stumbled forward, clattering clumsily on her skis, sagging with exhaustion and relief. She hadn't had time to clock who exactly had opened the door. She just felt herself being caught as she began toppling to the ground. Arms around her waist grabbed her, tugging her straight and then holding her upright, at which point she did take notice of the guy who was now supporting her.

Cold, narrowed eyes were staring down at her from a towering height. She was an unimpressive five-three and this guy was well over six feet. She blinked and the breath caught in her throat, because she was staring up at a man who was sinfully beautiful with perfectly chiselled features, sharp cheekbones, the oddest colour of green eyes and very dark, shortly cropped hair. He was wearing worn, faded jogging bottoms, an equally worn sweater and an expression of barely suppressed annoyance.

'What the hell are you doing here?'

'I…'

'You'd better come in, but only because I can't have you collapsing in a blizzard outside my front door!'

'I…'

'And you might as well bring the skis in too. Leave them out there and they'll be buried under the snow and, before you apologise for landing on my doorstep, I'll tell you straight away that the last thing I need is a complete stranger invading my privacy!'

Hard, green eyes bored into her and Alice, normally the sunniest of people, felt a quiver of anger. Today was definitely not her day when it came to letting her emotions get the better of her. She stood back, folded her arms and tried to ignore the bitter cold settling on her now that she was standing still.

'Well?' he demanded, scowling. 'You're letting the cold in.'

'I'm not sure I *want* to come in!' Alice shivered, her arms folded.

'What the hell are you going on about?'

'I don't like your attitude. I can't be too far from… from…civilisation, if you have a place here, and I'll take my chances if you point me in the right direction!'

'Don't be ridiculous!' He looked at her with even more narrow-eyed displeasure, then stared straight past her shoulder to the swirling snow now being consumed in darkness. 'Although…if you really want to take your chances? Approximately five miles south-east you might just stumble to the nearest very small town. Miss it, though, and you'll be spending a very cold night on the slopes and, despite your idiocy in being out here in the first place, my conscience won't let me send you on your way. So, if you still refuse to come in then I'll be forced to carry you in over my shoulder.'

'You wouldn't dare!'

'Care to try me?'

He spun round on his heels. Alice detached herself from her skis and tripped along hurriedly behind him, slamming the door behind her and breathing a sigh of blessed relief at the warmth that had replaced the biting cold.

She took a few seconds to glance around her. The place was cosy but utterly luxurious in an understated way. Wooden panelling and stained-glass windows splintered the fading light and the rug that covered the parquet floor was soft, faded and clearly silk. Two black-and-white photographs on the wall were signed by the photographer and looked vaguely familiar. She was ridding herself of her outer layers as he vanished into one of the rooms off to the right and, when she entered behind him, it was to find herself in a superbly fitted kitchen rich with smells that made her mouth water.

She cleared her throat and then reddened as he swung round to face her. The lighting in the hallway hadn't done him justice. Her mouth went dry as she took in his truly spectacular good looks. Her heart picked up speed and she frantically tried to get herself back to a place of righteous anger at his high-handed arrogance. Was she here on her own with him? she thought belatedly. Should she be concerned? What if he was dangerous? Strangely, she wasn't scared, but then again she was half-crazy with exhaustion, so her brain was probably not functioning properly.

'You're wet.'

His dark, cutting voice interrupted her wandering train of thought.

'That's because I've been out in a blizzard for hours. Okay, maybe not *hours*, but long enough.'

'Which is something I'll get to just as soon as you get out of those clothes.'

'I can't. I have nothing to put on. I forgot to travel with my suitcase.'

'You think this situation is funny?'

'No.' Alice had no idea what had come over her, because it wasn't like her to be sarcastic, and it certainly wasn't like her to be rude. 'And… I suppose I ought to thank you for letting me in to your house.'

'I had no choice.'

'Are you here…er…on your own?'

She blushed as his eyebrows winged upwards and he shot her a slow smile of cool amusement that transformed the sharp, arrogant edges of his face so that he went from drop-dead gorgeous to stupidly sexy.

'I'm afraid so,' he drawled. 'Absolutely no handy chaperones in the form of wife and kids but, before you have a fainting fit, I can assure you that you're one hundred percent safe with me. I couldn't be less interested in some fool who's ventured out in a blizzard thinking that it might be a bit of a challenge. Follow me.'

'Follow you?'

'You'll have to borrow some of my clothes.'

Alice laughed incredulously. She couldn't help it. 'You really think I'm going to fit into anything you have here?'

'You'll have to use your ingenuity,' he said, pausing right in front of her, close enough for her pick up the clean, woody masculine scent of whatever aftershave he was wearing. 'Spending more time in wet clothes isn't an option.'

'No,' Alice replied, hackles rising again. 'I suppose getting a bout of flu and ending up bedridden is only slightly less troublesome for you than me getting lost in a blizzard in search of a small town somewhere further down the slopes.'

'You said it.'

'That's not very nice!'

'I do "honest" over "nice".'

'I'd never have guessed.' She met his impassive stare and then sighed. 'I'm sorry. I'm being very rude, and that's not like me. Of course I'll borrow some of your clothes. I don't want to get ill because I'm too proud to accept your help.'

She smiled with genuine, tentative warmth. Why was she reacting to him like this—as though he had reached deep into part of her she hadn't known existed and turned on a switch that had sent her emotions into some weird, puzzling place? He was a perfect stranger, for heaven's sake!

Even when she had broken up with Simon, she had done so in a calm, measured way. They had talked. She had been upset, but she hadn't felt out of control; feeling out of control just wasn't in her DNA. She wasn't cutting or sarcastic by nature. She had grown up in a vicarage and had learnt from a young age to be thoughtful of other people.

Over the years there had been many, many broken people who had dropped in to see her father, who was the kindest man on the planet. She had learnt to be patient and to listen to whatever they wanted to say if her father happened to be busy at the time and hadn't been able to see them straightaway. She had sat serenely though more gossip about who was doing what to the flower arrangements than she could shake a stick at.

She was equable by nature. Escaping from the chalet to think had been impulsive for her, but maybe the conversation about engagements had tapped into a depth of regret she really hadn't known was there.

At any rate, the way she was reacting to this guy was a completely alien to her. Was it because he was so good-looking, so arrogant? So unlike any guy she had ever met in her life before? Had she surrounded herself so much with *ordinary* that this guy, so far away from ordinary, unsettled her in ways she couldn't deal with?

'I think it's time for introductions,' Mateo said gruffly. He shoved his hands in the pockets of the joggers, dragging them down just a bit so that now they rode low on his hips, and tilted his head to the side.

A woman, banging on his front door, criticising his attitude even though he'd *rescued* her from a blizzard by letting her in in the first place? Not at all what he had been expecting. He was so accustomed to obedience, and so tuned in to women who were always eager to please, that he had been lost for words at the sheer nerve of this unexpected intruder blown in on the wind.

Even more annoying for Mateo was the fact that there

was an appeal to her that bypassed his justifiable displeasure at her presence in his chalet, in his *sanctuary*. She'd followed him into the kitchen and he turned around to a curvy little sex kitten who had stripped down to her thermal layers, none of which could quite conceal the fullness of her breasts or the narrow handspan of her waist. She'd also dragged off the woolly hat to reveal a spill of long copper curls that tangled over her shoulders and made the breath catch in his throat.

He was in danger of staring, and that was a reaction that was both foreign and unacceptable to him. Mateo's life was highly controlled. As far as he was concerned, surprises were rarely welcome, particularly when it came to the opposite sex. No surprises at all really worked for him. He went for women who fitted a mould: leggy blondes who enjoyed all the things that money could buy and, even more, all the doors that a powerful guy like him could open: doors to a social scene that tended to bore him but usually thrilled them to death. They demanded no more than he was willing to provide: fun without commitment.

Right now, Mateo was taking a breather from relationships of any kind, so it was intensely irritating to find his eyes being drawn to a woman who wasn't even anything like the ones he usually invited into his life. Said woman was currently looking at him with guarded eyes, waiting for him to introduce himself, as opposed to standing and staring like an idiot.

'I'm Mateo. And you are…?'

'Alice. Alice Reynolds.'

'Right. Now that we've covered that, I'll get some

clothes for you and show you to the bathroom…' He paused and raked his fingers through his hair as she continued to look at him with huge, almond-shaped hazel eyes that somehow managed to dredge up something inside him that had no place in his tough, aggressive personality.

'Look, I get that you might be a little alarmed at being in a strange place with a guy you don't know, and I don't want to be flippant about that—you're perfectly safe here. There's not much I can add to that; you'll just have to trust me on that front. You haven't told me what you're doing in this part of the world, or who you've come with, but I have excellent connectivity here, and if you let me have your phone I can connect you so you can get in touch with whoever's out there rustling up a search party to hunt you down.'

'Oh! Would you believe that hadn't even crossed my mind? Yes, please, that would be great.'

She smiled a smile of such open radiance that Mateo was temporarily knocked off his feet but he concealed it well. She was fumbling to fetch her phone and he deliberately didn't spare her a distracted sideways glance as he connected her to his Wi-Fi and then brushed past her to his suite, sensing her light tread behind him and trying hard not to conjure up her image in his head.

'I just want to say…'

He paused and glanced round to find her standing inches away from him, face upturned and still smiling.

'Yes?' he muttered gruffly.

'I just want to say that I know you don't want me here.' She grimaced and rolled her eyes, laughing at herself. 'Even if you hadn't said so yourself, I can tell that I've interrupted whatever down time you had planned, and I'm sorry about that. I'm afraid I was a little rude when I first…well…fell headlong into your chalet but I honestly had no idea the weather was going to turn when I set off earlier. I was so scared out there… I guess my head was all over the place!'

'That's…fine.'

'And then I made it here and I was just so relieved that I wasn't going to die out there on the slopes that I didn't even stop to consider that…that… I mean, you could have been *anyone*!'

'I… Yes, I suppose I could have been.' Mateo was fascinated by this long, meandering explanation which wasn't designed to grab his attention or capture his interest. He was so accustomed to coy advances that her open honesty was a little disorienting.

'You read about these things. And then there are all the movies…'

'You do read about those things and, yes, I suppose there are movies out there as well, although I don't do them. Look, I'll fetch some stuff for you. You can choose whatever you want, and if you leave your wet things on the floor of the bathroom I'll stick them in the machine.'

'That's very kind. I can't believe I ever thought you might have been an axe-murderer.'

'You thought I might have been an *axe-murderer*?' Mateo stared at her and she smiled back, blushing and sheepish.

'Like I said, I've seen enough movies in my time, although I guess the typical axe-murderer wouldn't rent a chalet like this…although, in fairness, perhaps I'm stereotyping axe-murderers.'

'I happen to own this!'

'Which makes the axe-murderer scenario even more implausible. And yet…did you say that you *don't do movies*? I didn't know there was anyone who *didn't* do movies.'

'We should continue this conversation…eh…later. Now, there are three suites here so you can use either of the two spare and you can take your time…eh…freshening up. No need to join me for dinner if you'd rather go to sleep. I imagine your nerves are frayed.'

'Actually, I'm quite hungry.' She cast her eyes downward and then glanced back up at him and blushed. 'I keep meaning to go on a diet but somehow that never really gets off the ground.'

Mateo backed away as the silence thickened. She'd brought his attention bounding back to her shapely little body and he was perspiring as he reached the door and nodded in the direction of the bedroom suites off the broad landing.

His eyes flicked to her semi-damp layer that stretched lovingly over her generous breasts and sexy curves. He swallowed…and scowled.

'Right. I'll be in the kitchen.'

He left without further pointless pleasantries. He wished he could summon up the suffocating impatience he had felt when he had pulled that door open. Instead, the woman seemed to have distracted him, and as he stalked back to the kitchen, glowering at his momentary lapse in focus, the reality of the situation sank in.

His peace had been invaded. God only knew when the blizzard would stop but certainly he would be stuck with her for the next day, possibly more. And, instead of trying to think of ways in which he could somehow confine her to safe quarters so that they weren't actually sharing space, he was already resigning himself to the fact that that was going to be impossible. Worse, he wasn't quite sure whether that was a problem for him or not.

He returned to the business of cooking but his solitude had been interrupted. Images of her filled his head and he loathed that. Truth was, there were things that were contained within him, experiences best left buried. They'd remain buried just so long as his life didn't derail, but the appearance of one Alice Reynolds had derailed him completely. As he stirred the sauce, his disobedient mind wandered back to his youth and to memories usually kept under lock and key.

Mateo had been nineteen when he'd met Bianca. He'd been within touching distance of getting his degree a year and a half ahead of schedule. She'd shown up at one of his boxing matches and had knocked him sideways with her beauty. What red-blooded teenager could have resisted all that long, dark hair, flashing dark eyes and a mouth that had invited a world of sexual adventure?

He'd fallen hook, line and sinker…for about six months, before realising that no amount of hot sex could detract from the cold reality that the two of them were not suited. He'd had ambitions; he'd wanted to move on from website designing for other people to ruling the world single-handedly. He'd known it would take time but that he would get there. He'd been young, ambitious and insanely clever.

She'd wanted the fast riches to be made if he turned professional as a boxer. She'd craved the adrenaline that would have come with the limelight and the lifestyles of the crowd that might hang around him. She'd been impatient, and contemptuous when it had come to looking at the bigger picture and thinking long-term.

The body he'd lusted after had begun to bore him and his eyes had begun to wander. The happiness he'd felt when she walked through the door had turned to irritation and impatience.

On the brink of breaking up, she'd fallen pregnant and everything then had changed. Mateo had married her. He'd been just twenty with a baby on the way and all his dreams of making it big in the world of start-ups and finance had started to dissolve, like dew on a summer's morning. Money had had to be made there and then and turning professional would have paid all the bills and more. Bianca might not have been right for him but he'd been determined to put his all into a baby he'd found himself secretly thrilled to have fathered.

He'd never know how that adventure might have turned out because a miscarriage at a little over three months into the pregnancy had thrown everything up in the air. They'd stayed together for another eight months. He, because he'd felt sorry for her, had seen it as his duty to stand by her at a time when she'd needed him, whatever his personal feelings; and because, for a while, he'd been crippled by a sadness he hadn't expected, adrift and unable to think straight. And Bianca, yes: she'd been upset, and had clung just for a while, but she was tough and essentially narcissistic.

'We can always have another; we're young,' she'd told him with casual insouciance. The thought of a lifestyle being married to a professional boxer still glittered for her like a treasure chest waiting to be opened. Not for a single moment had she doubted that he would continue on that track. It wasn't to be, and he'd been relieved when she'd finally walked out on him because he'd told her to forget it if she thought he was going to launch into a career in which he had no interest.

Mateo frowned now and resigned himself to the fact that his wayward mind was just going to carry on travelling down memory lane. Maybe releasing pent-up thoughts wasn't such a bad thing. Maybe every so often he needed to pull them out from whatever vault he'd stashed them in and examine them, remind himself why he was the person he was—someone who would never take on commitment again or think that love was something that actually existed.

Maybe it paid sometimes, such as when a perfect stranger somehow put him on the back foot, to remember the ex-wife who had resurfaced five years after their divorce to try and squeeze money out of him. He'd been on the up and she'd been pregnant with another man's baby but that hadn't stopped her from trying to emotionally blackmail him into handing over money to her.

He was just managing to get back in control, and beginning to be just a little amused by his own temporary bout of introspection, when he heard Alice clear her throat from behind him. He turned round to see her standing in the doorway and this time she wasn't in tight, wet ski gear. No snug thermals were lovingly stretched across a body that was sex on legs.

She was wearing his clothes and it felt incredibly intimate. He felt a rush of blood to his head as he looked at her from under lowered lashes. She wore black joggers, and a striped jumper, everything rolled, cuffed and tugged tight, yet still swamping her.

Jesus.

He felt faint.

'Smells delicious…and thank you for the clothes. Not quite my size but I actually feel like a human being again.'

Mateo watched as she smiled and edged into the kitchen, all tension from earlier gone as a naturally upbeat nature was revealed. He was lost for words.

'Sit.' It was more of a command than he'd intended and he flushed darkly. 'Make yourself at home,' he countered roughly. 'And then you can begin to tell me what brings you to this part of the world—by which I mean the wrong side of the mountain.'

He reminded himself that this wasn't a social visit and he wasn't playing the part of Prince Charming looking for the owner of a glass slipper. She'd landed on his doorstep through her own foolish risk-taking, and in so doing had interrupted his very much anticipated time-out here.

'Because, just in case you didn't know,' he went on, 'This part of Mont Blanc takes no prisoners. For future reference, it's easy to end up a casualty of nature here unless you happen to be an experienced skier.'

'And I will duly remember your words of warning.' She gave that smile again, this time pretending and failing to be contrite. Mateo frowned, irritated to be taken off-guard once again.

'I promise: Scout's honour. And now, before I explain why I ended up banging on your door, let me help you do something. I may not be the best cook in the world but I'm a dab hand when it comes to chopping stuff.'

She walked towards him and Mateo looked at her narrowly, taking in everything and finding it difficult to drag his gaze away.

CHAPTER TWO

'I CAN HANDLE ONIONS.'

'There's no need for you to earn your keep by helping, Alice. Sit, relax—recover from your ordeal.'

'Honestly, I like to help out.' Alice smiled when she thought about her parents. She had grown up with people coming and going; helping out wherever and whenever was ingrained in her, which was probably why she had become a teacher. She enjoyed kids, and enjoyed the business of having a job where she felt she might be making a real difference. 'Now that we've established that you're not an axe-murderer,' she teased playfully, 'can you tell me what you do?'

Out of the corner of her eye she could see his hands, strong and bronzed, as he expertly continued to prepare whatever meal he had been preparing before she had ruined his peace.

'I… I'm self-employed, you could say.'

'That's tough, but you're obviously good at what you do, if you can afford a chalet out here.'

'Tough?'

'I'd hate the insecurity—never knowing where your

next meal is coming from. I teach. It's the most secure job in the world.' Her eyes were beginning to water and she blinked and stepped back a bit.

'You're a teacher? Shouldn't you be at a school somewhere?'

'Half-term; I'm here with three friends. I can't tell you how relieved they were to hear from me! Anyway, we've been planning this trip for ages, and just going back to when you told me about being an idiot for skiing on this side of the mountain…'

She grimaced and looked sideways at him. 'I'm actually a pretty experienced skier,' she confessed, resuming her work on the onions, but half-heartedly, because she was so conscious of him next to her. She was buzzing with curiosity but knew better than to indulge it. Whoever he was and whatever he did, he didn't seem to be the sort of open, talkative guy she was used to. She felt way out of her comfort zone just being around him and that was weirdly exciting. She wondered whether she was getting on his nerves with her chat but then what else was she supposed to do? She was talkative by nature and the thought of standing there in a state of repressed silence filled her with horror.

Actually, she just didn't think she could do it.

'I taught skiing on these very slopes for six months… Well, not *these* very ones—the easier runs on the other side—before I started my teacher training course.'

'Right.'

'So I'm accustomed to difficult runs but that blizzard just dropped out of the sky like a snow bomb. By the time it hit, there was no one else around on the slopes.'

* * *

'Perhaps they'd wisely noticed the darkening skies, because I'm really struggling to believe that a blizzard can strike within seconds. Somehow that seems to defy the laws of nature.'

'That's a possibility,' Alice conceded thoughtfully. She paused and then swivelled so that she was leaning against the counter, her hazel eyes pensive as she stared off into the distance. 'I'm normally really clued up when it comes to changes out here but…my mind was a million miles away. What seemed sudden may not have been quite as sudden as I thought.'

Mateo took over the onions. He looked down at her, primed to discourage any unwelcome outpouring of personal back-stories, but hesitated at the expression on her face, which was a mixture of sadness and resignation.

Something in his gut made him think that she was too young and too inherently upbeat to be sad and resigned. Suddenly he felt a hundred years old. He was thirty-three. He couldn't be more than a handful of years older than her but he felt jaded, cynical and ancient.

He knew how that had happened, and knew that there was nothing wrong with being cynical, because cynicism was a great self-defence mechanism. But for the first time he uneasily wondered what another road might have looked like. Disillusionment and the bitterness of divorce had taught him the value of being tough and keeping out the world, but what would that world have looked like if he had kept doors open to it? The openness of the woman looking at him seemed to encourage restless thoughts that had no place in his life.

Impatient with himself, he told her to go and sit.

'There's not much left to do,' he said shortly. 'Dinner will be ready in half an hour.'

'Okay.'

'And help yourself to more wine.'

He'd opened a bottle of red and poured them both a glass. She'd sipped her way through half of hers.

'I'm annoying you, aren't I?'

'What sort of question is that?' Mateo turned to look at her. She had subsided into one of the chairs at the table, a small thing bundled in clothing too big for her, nursing her glass and staring mournfully in his direction.

'I don't suppose you expected to end up having to cook food for someone you don't want in your chalet.'

'Life throws curve balls.'

'You don't strike me as the sort who does curve balls. A bit like you don't do movies.'

'Come again?'

'Doesn't matter.' Alice shrugged. 'I don't blame you for being annoyed that you're stuck with me. Hopefully this blizzard will die down tomorrow and I can be on my way.' She rose to stroll towards the bank of windows and peered through the wooden shutters that concealed the vast space outside. 'Doesn't look like it,' she said on a sigh. 'When you're in here, you don't think it's as wild outside as it is.'

'Your friends…' Mateo said awkwardly, sipping his wine and staring at her over the rim of his glass but remaining where he was, leaning against the counter, keeping a safe distance between them. He didn't like the way he was distracted by her. 'Is one of them your partner? If so, no need to be depressed about it. I'm sure this will blow over and I'll make sure you're safely delivered back to your lodge.'

'Thank you. I'm an excellent skier; I certainly don't need to be delivered anywhere safely by you! The days of damsels in distress needing to be rescued by knights in shining armour, who think they're better skiers than they are, are long over.' She grinned.

Mateo shot her a reluctant smile. He was tempted to tell her that he couldn't think of any woman who would have rejected his offer and a lot who would have tried to engineer that exact situation. However, something told him that any comment along those lines wouldn't go down well, which made the temptation to voice it even stronger.

'But what about the anxious boyfriend wringing his hands and waiting for you to show up? Is he as experienced a skier as you?'

Food ready, Mateo began bringing dishes to the table, proud of the way he had risen to the occasion without resentment and only a little bit of initial hostility. The woman might have something about her he found a little unsettling, but it hadn't put too much of a dent in his basic manners. He'd stepped up to the plate and not allowed his own personal annoyance at her invasion of his privacy get the better of him.

He wondered whether it helped that she was so straightforward and not interested in him as anything other than someone who had come to her aid. Maybe her sheer novelty value had lowered his defences, or maybe the unexpected situation had in turn generated unexpected reactions—unwelcome, uninvited but oddly energising, intoxicating reactions.

Alice's stomach rumbled. She didn't want to appear rude but she honestly couldn't wait to dive into what he had produced from some onions, tomatoes and other bits and pieces that would probably have confounded her. Her culinary skills were basic to say the least. She watched as he helped her to the breaded chicken and pasta in a sauce that made her mouth water. She saw a shadow of a smile on his face.

'That's quite enough,' she said hurriedly. 'I couldn't possibly eat any more.'

'What about some cheese?'

Alice hesitated. He was here on his own and he wasn't wearing a wedding ring, not that that meant much. But was there a girlfriend in the background somewhere—even a wife? Whoever he was going out with, she was pretty sure that person wouldn't have wanted to tuck into a plate piled high with food topped with a generous dollop of fresh parmesan on top.

'Okay but just a bit. For the record, I'm here with three girlfriends. I… I don't have an anxious boyfriend waiting for me anywhere.'

'So what propelled you to make a headlong dash to this side of the mountain without your friends?' He shot her an astute look that was discomforting, because it seemed to bore straight into her. 'If I were the sort to indulge in guessing games, I'd have said you would have shot down here because of boyfriend troubles.'

'I...'

'Not that I'm asking you to expand,' Mateo interjected smoothly. 'Your business.'

Alice reddened, again in the grip of embarrassment at the thought that she was boring him.

He was making polite chit-chat because he had no choice. The last thing he wanted to hear was about her life or about *her*.

'What about you?' she asked, going slowly with the food, which took a lot of willpower, because she was ravenous. 'I mean, why are you here on your own? Do *you* have anyone waiting up for you?'

'I don't believe my private life is any of your business,' he returned gently.

'It's not. But if you can ask questions about me then isn't it only fair that I ask questions about you?'

'Not entirely, considering this is my lodge and you happen to be in it through misfortune as opposed to invitation.'

'That's not a very nice thing to say!'

'I've sometimes been told that I'm not a very nice person,' Mateo returned with a shrug.

'Have you?'

'You sound shocked.' He grinned at her and Alice felt her skin prickle and a tide of pink wash her face.

'Don't you care?'

'No.' He raised his eyebrows, still smiling. 'But, moving on from that, like I said when you got here, no wife and no girlfriend. Not here or waiting anywhere for me.'

Alice sighed. 'You're a fantastic cook.' She changed the subject but was itching to return to him, to find out more about him, even though he was perfectly right to say that it was hardly her business to probe into his private life, as someone who had infuriatingly landed on his doorstep like a parcel delivered to the wrong address. She didn't even know what he did: 'self-employed' could cover a multitude of sins!

'What are you self-employed doing?' she couldn't resist asking. 'And I know it's none of my business, because I'm just here through sheer bad luck—at least, bad luck *for you*. Good luck for me.'

Mateo burst out laughing and pushed his plate to one side so that he could relax back in the chair and look at her, head tilted to one side.

'You have a way when it comes to asking questions.'

'Maybe it's because I'm a teacher. We're kind of trained to ask questions. So, what do you do? Are you a ski-instructor?'

He laughed again, this time with more amusement, and carried on looking at her, his amazing eyes as intimate as a caress as they rested on her.

'From axe-murderer to ski-instructor with nothing in between.'

'You told me you're self-employed and you… Well, you have a chalet here out on one of the more dangerous runs, so you must be an experienced skier. I'm putting two and two together.'

'You should avoid a career as a detective. No, I'm not

a ski instructor, as it happens, even if I am proficient on the skis. I work in…tech.'

'Oh.'

'You look disappointed.'

'I always thought that IT people were geeky.'

'Not all.'

Mateo lowered his lashes.

Was this what it felt like to be anonymous, to blend in with the crowd and inhabit a place where no one around you knew who you were?

It was a long time since he'd been in that position. For most of his adult life, as he'd climbed the ladder at dizzying speed, he had become a recognisable commodity. He realised his world had shrunk to contain only people who moved in the same circles as he did. It was safe. Was it also limiting? It was something he hadn't really considered before, because 'safe' equalled 'controlled' and control appealed.

Wealth and power attracted wealth and power and, while he had never courted any social scene, social scenes courted him. He got invitations to prominent events: hobnobbing with the great and the good; parties for openings stuffed with celebrities; and of course all those essential networking dos where the rich and influential mixed with the other rich and influential.

This getaway here was a taste of sanity. Being here with her meant she had no idea who he was and that was beginning to feel a little like a taste of sanity: stolen… temporary…pleasurable. She might not be his type. He definitely didn't go for fluffy, small, voluptuous women who talked a lot, but he could write a book on the appeal of the unpredictable.

All taboo, when he thought about it. He shook himself free of the disturbing feeling of control slipping through his fingers.

'So no argument with your boyfriend has brought you here,' Mateo inserted briskly. 'You were overcome with a need for some fresh air.'

'Not as such.'

'What does that mean?'

He opened his mouth to tell her again that he didn't care whether she confided in him or not, that in fact he would rather she didn't, but some base-level curiosity got the better of him and he shot her an encouraging look.

'Well,' Alice confided in a hitched voice. 'My friend announced her engagement with lots of fanfare and champagne-cork-popping and I…well… I guess it just got to me. I was engaged eight months ago and… I broke it off. It's not as though I'm sad that it ended, but all of a sudden I just felt empty inside and I had to get away. So, when I say the blizzard swept in from nowhere, it might have been a case of being so lost in my thoughts that I didn't notice the sky getting darker and the snow getting thicker. At least, not until it was too late to do anything about it.'

Mateo shifted because, generally speaking, he disliked all this touchy-feely stuff. But then frowned as he saw tears begin to gather in the corner of her eyes. He hastily scouted round for something useful and settled on some paper towels on the kitchen counter, which he pushed over to her.

'If you ditched the guy then why are you shedding tears over him? It obviously wasn't much of a relationship.'

'How can you say that?' Alice rounded on him and vigorously dabbed her eyes.

'You dumped him.'

'Doesn't mean—'

'Doesn't mean what?'

'Doesn't mean it didn't hurt. Simon and I went back a long way. I'd known him since I was fifteen! He should have been the ideal guy for me.'

'Mmm.'

'What's that supposed to mean?'

Mateo shrugged. 'I'm the last person qualified to give advice on the makings of a good relationship, but if you'd known the guy since you were a kid, then maybe it was all just a little too cosy. Cosy,' he said wryly, 'is just a cousin once removed from boring, and who wants a boring partner?'

He looked at her with guarded appreciation and a little voice whispered to him, *what would it be like, this woman who is so different from anyone else you've ever known...?*

He shifted and cleared his head of the treacherous thought. It just didn't pay to have thoughts like that. Bianca had been *different* once upon a time, until she'd ended up being just the same.

'Simon was far from boring.'

'So did the excitement get too much for you?'

'I don't know why I bothered to say anything to you about this,' Alice muttered.

She met his gaze with fierce resistance but was thrown by the cool, amused, all-knowing, *worldly* look in the green eyes resting on her.

What must he think of her? She shouldn't care but suddenly she saw herself through his eyes: small, could lose a few pounds, way too talkative and willing to confide, even in the face of all his signals that he was not that interested.

He might be an IT nerd but, with his looks, she reckoned he could have anyone he wanted, and from what she had seen of his chalet he was also not living in penury. He was one of those IT nerds with cash and those were in high demand. So was it any surprise that he found her *amusing*, after his initial horror that she had ruined his holiday for one? He didn't see her as *a woman*. He saw her as a novelty toy: wind her up and watch her go. At least, that was her suspicion, and it was making her self-conscious.

'I'm sorry,' he surprised her by saying quietly. 'I don't mean to make fun of you or to somehow belittle what you've been through. It must have been tough, breaking off an engagement...'

'It was,' Alice said, drawn once again into his orbit and seduced into opening up, because there was something so compelling about him. 'Everyone expected us to end up together, and I felt awful, because Simon is the nicest guy in the world.'

But just a tiny bit boring, she thought with a rare flash of acerbity. *Way too cosy...way too much of a known quantity...* 'I know what you're going to say.'

'Do you? Enlighten me.'

'You're going to say that *nice* equals *boring*.'

'Ah, was I? Thank you for filling me in. Saves me the bother of saying anything.'

'You wouldn't understand. I bet you've never experienced a broken engagement before—never known what it was like to pin your hopes on something, only for it to dissolve at the last minute.'

The silence that greeted this stretched and stretched until Alice began to fidget and wonder whether an apology might not be in order, although it wasn't as though she'd asked him anything personal or been in any way offensive. He'd glanced down but now, as he raised his eyes to hers, they were cool and remote.

'Can I ask something?'

'What?' Alice said cautiously.

'How old are you?'

'Twenty-four.'

'Don't you think you're very young to be thinking about embarking on love, marriage and the whole nine yards?'

Alice thought about her happily married parents, having met when they'd still been teenagers going to the same school. There had been a brief separation when they had gone to different universities but breaking up had never occurred to them.

She uneasily wondered whether she had thrown herself into Simon in a subconscious desire to emulate the example her parents had set. Or had she just been lazy in following a path that had been set for her without examining whether that was *her* path?

'You're never too young to fall in love,' she said vaguely.

'But you didn't, did you? You made a mistake.'

'Well…'

'Not my problem. But, if you want to take some advice from someone a little further down the road than you, then I would say forget about the "true love" business at the moment. You have your life ahead of you; plenty of leg room to see what's out there before you go looking for whatever it is you're looking for.'

'See what's out there?'

'Have fun and forget about the love,' Mateo murmured in a low, silky voice that made the hairs on the back of her neck stand on end.

Have fun… I bet you'd be a lot of fun…

The thought leapt out at her with such surprising force that she was briefly struck dumb. She stared at him, her colour mounting, taking in the perfect symmetry of his face, his blatant sexuality and the lazy drift of his eyes that never left her face.

Surely he wasn't flirting with her? That would be highly inappropriate, she decided.

At this point she felt that a jolt of alarm was in order. She should rise to her feet and say something about feeling tired and needing to get some rest. He wouldn't stop her because, if there was one thing her gut instinct told her, it was that this guy was a gentleman, despite the arrogant, self-assured veneer and the annoying way he had of getting under her skin by telling her stuff she didn't want to hear.

Instead, a buzz of forbidden excitement anchored her to the chair and she felt her pulse begin to pick up pace. Her body felt sensitive under the baggy clothes, *his* baggy clothes.

She fidgeted and then kept very still, just in case he noticed.

'I'll certainly have fun,' she said politely.

'Want some cheese? It's the only dessert I eat.'

'You have a lot of dos and don'ts in your life, don't you?'

'What do you mean?'

Mateo was efficient when it came to tidying up behind himself. One more didn't add much to the process. He brought three packs of exotic soft cheeses out of the fridge, along with crackers from the cupboard, and could tell that she was sorely tempted to join him but for some reason had decided that she would be ladylike and refuse.

How was she to know that he liked the way she enjoyed her food? He was also surprising himself with his tolerance when it came to her airing her views about this, that and everything under the sun, despite the fact that she surely must have read the room and noted that he was not the most encouraging person in the world when it came to people sharing their opinions *of* him *with* him. In fact, thinking about it, hadn't he already made that perfectly clear on a couple of occasions?

'I mean…' Mateo watched with interest as she leant forward. Her arms were resting on the table and her breasts were nestled on her arms. They were abundant enough to push against the baggy clothes and it was making his imagination go into overdrive. 'Mmm…?'

he encouraged absently as he felt the stirring of an erection. It was disobeying everything it was being told to do, namely to stop saluting and stand down.

She leant forward a little more. He wondered what she would look like under his clothes: rosy nipples, taut, tender and waiting to be kissed; the weight of heavy breasts in his big hands; the glorious perfection of wet womanhood opening up to him like a flower...

He drew in a sharp breath and sank a little lower in his chair.

'You don't do movies.' She ticked off each point on her fingers in a very prim manner that was also something of a turn-on. 'You don't do dessert, which means you probably don't do chocolate or ice-cream; you clearly don't do sharing of confidences, and you probably don't do love and marriage either, because you prefer to have fun, no strings attached...'

'I admit that's a fair summary of me.' He grinned. 'There *are*, however, quite a few things that I *do* do.' He relaxed in the chair and realised that he was thoroughly enjoying himself. He took his time sampling some of the Brie and then pushed it over to Alice, gratified when she distractedly wedged some off with one of the crackers. He vaguely thought that it would be highly satisfying to take her to one of the terrific restaurants he went to in London and have her sample some of the finest food the capital had to offer. Not, he reminded himself, that that was on the cards.

'I *do*...' he tabulated on his fingers '...work hard and I *do*...' he looked at her from under sooty, long lashes '...play hard.'

Thickening silence greeted this remark. Mateo noted the heightened colour that stole into her cheeks. She had a wonderfully transparent face, devoid of all artifice and guile. It wasn't just the way she looked, though. It wasn't just the satiny smoothness of her skin, the luminosity of her hazel eyes or the fact that her perfect hourglass figure did something crazy to his libido.

Her appeal lay in more than that. She dared to be one hundred percent genuine around him and that was a novelty. She didn't play games—maybe because she didn't know who he was, but he wanted to think that she just wasn't a game player. He could spot those a mile off, whatever tactics they used and he could deal with them. In many ways, game players were a known quantity and when you were a billionaire, he figured they came with the territory. The woman who had just given him a stern critique of his failings was unique in all her differences.

He could tell from her expression that he had embarrassed her. Most women at this point would have fallen over themselves to explore his ambiguous rejoinder. She, however, was looking at him as though he had suddenly decided to do a striptease without warning her in advance.

'Apologies.' He held up his hands in a gesture of rueful surrender, belying the fact that his erection was still as hard as steel. 'Just a thoughtless, light-hearted remark.'

'No! No, no, no! Of *course* I understand that. When you're freelance and having to work every day to get a pay packet, because if you have a day off you don't get paid, then you need to let your hair down now and again.'

'My life isn't exactly that tortured.' Mateo had the decency to flush at this sweeping misunderstanding of his position in life. He could frankly walk away from it all tomorrow and still have enough money to cruise through life in a way most people could only dream of doing.

'And I can also understand,' Alice said with bald sincerity, 'why you were so annoyed when I banged on your door and you were forced to let me in, a complete stranger.'

'You can…?'

'You probably don't get heaps of time off.'

'I do work long hours, now that you mention it.'

'So you get your one week here, or maybe two, and it's interrupted by me. Can I ask…where is your permanent home?'

'I…' Mateo opened his mouth to say what came naturally to him, which was that he had several places. Although, he might be hard pushed to call any of them *home*, as such, which implied open fires and a dog somewhere, along with a partner waiting for him every evening with a hot meal and his slippers at the ready. 'I live in London.'

Her face lit up.

'So do I!' She looked at him sympathetically. 'I guess you probably don't live in the sort of place I live in.' She smiled without rancour. 'If you can afford this as a holiday home then you're not broke, which is good. Poverty can be a burden that pushes many off the cliff edge.'

'I guess you could say that I'm not penniless.' Mateo's

antennae vibrated because the last thing he wanted was to get involved in a discussion about what he could or couldn't afford, even though he could see that she was utterly guileless in her questioning. A fundamental caring nature shone through everything she said. It was fascinating. The world he inhabited was dog-eat-dog and the women he dated enjoyed the challenge of dating a guy who lived in the fast lane. Right now he could be talking to someone from another planet.

'Or maybe you rent this place out when you're not using it? That would pay the overheads...'

'Indeed.'

'And then gives you enough to have somewhere modest, because honestly, getting onto the property ladder in London is a nightmare, isn't it?'

'Total nightmare.' He thought of his six-bedroomed house in Holland Park with its manicured gardens in the front and rear and its own gym and swimming pool in the basement.

'I have no idea whether I'll ever be able to afford anything bigger than a box on my salary.' She sighed. 'Anyway, I get you value your time here, and didn't want it interrupted.'

'Well,' Mateo mused silkily, 'now that it has been, I must tell you that I'm finding it far less onerous than I ever thought possible...'

CHAPTER THREE

THE BLIZZARD ABATED but the snow kept falling, a steady sheet of never-ending white.

They stood outside surveying the scene.

He'd washed her stuff so she could get back into her thermals but, rather than don the whole ensemble when she wouldn't be going anywhere near her skis, Alice had opted to wear some more of Mateo's clothes. She tugged the sleeves of the jumper to cover her balled fists but, despite all the layers, five seconds outside made her exposed skin pinch with cold. Next to her, she could feel Mateo's warmth and the unsettling power of his proximity.

The night before seemed like a dream. Had she imagined the frisson that had shimmered between them, tantalising and forbidden? She remembered landing on his doorstep like an unwanted package. She remembered how antagonistic he had been when he'd opened the door and found her outside. He hadn't been downright hostile, but he'd made it clear that she wasn't wanted, that he was only taking her in because there was no alternative. On a scale of one to ten, his welcome had scored a paltry four.

His attitude should have got her back up but somehow he'd managed to get under her skin, even though he hadn't made the slightest effort to charm. She remembered all that.

But had she *misremembered* the way the evening had progressed? Of course, she'd talked too much; that was just who she was. She'd talked and laughed, wine had been poured and his attitude had relaxed. He'd obviously chosen to go down the pragmatic road of accepting the inevitable with as good a grace as humanly possible Those cool, green eyes had rested on her... and that was when it all got a little blurry. Had she imagined a flicker of heat there? Had she imagined a thread of electricity that had ignited between them, sizzling quietly under the patter of their conversation like a firecracker?

He worked hard and he played hard...

She remembered that and she remembered wondering whether he'd been flirting with her, just for that second. It was all so *blurry*. What *wasn't* blurry was the thought that had followed her to sleep and wakened her in the morning, and that was the realisation that something about the man *excited* her.

She didn't know why but he did. She'd woken groggily a couple of hours earlier and had lain perfectly still for a few minutes, indulging in a bout of utter mortification that she might just have made a fool of herself the evening before.

Had she misread signals that hadn't been there and said anything that could have been misinterpreted? She wasn't used to alcohol and she couldn't quite remember how much she'd drunk. On the plus side, she hadn't fallen off her chair in a drunken stupor. On the minus side, she just might have stared at him a little too avidly, like a star-struck teenager, or worse—a desperate woman craving attention from a good-looking guy, having just recovered from a broken engagement. She might have attempted to flirt, having misinterpreted something said in jest.

By the time she'd dressed and left the room, she'd decided that the best route forward while she was stuck here—because one glance outside her window had killed any hope of heading back to her chalet today—was to pretend that the evening before hadn't happened. To have no blurry memories of sparks that might or might not have been there. No trying to wade through and analyse whatever conversation they had had. No wondering whether he had flirted with her. And no constant chatting and over-sharing.

She had been unnaturally quiet as they had shared breakfast, and had politely insisted on doing the dishes while he'd dealt with whatever early-morning emails it seemed he had to do. When he had resurfaced an hour later, again with stunning politeness she had agreed that they should check what was happening outside.

It had been draining.

At any rate, here they were now, and she shivered and glanced sideways at him.

Unfairly, he was as devastatingly handsome this morning as he had been the day before. That was one instance where, unfortunately, her imagination had not been playing tricks on her.

'At least the wind's died down,' she said.

'Still snowing pretty hard, though.'

'It's a shame. I'd hoped it might have abated over-night.' She wondered whether anyone ever spoke like that, using words such as 'abated'. *She* certainly didn't; it felt unnatural. 'I'd hoped,' she continued, 'that I might have been able to ski back to my chalet this morning, and enjoy the rest of my holiday with my friends instead of being cooped up here, but I'm not entirely sure that's going to happen.'

'We should head back inside. No point freezing to death out here chit-chatting about how heavy the snow is.'

'Indeed,' Alice heard herself say.

He headed in and she followed, watching him as he preceded her and, much as she didn't want to, appreciating the lithe grace of his body as he cut a path through the snow to his front door, making it easy for her to follow in his footsteps.

He was in black: black roll-neck jumper, black jogging bottoms and a black waterproof which he wore with careless elegance.

If she'd made the mistake of flirting with him the evening before, then Lord knew he'd probably spent the night roaring with laughter in his head. Even if he did something as boring as work in tech, he was so good-looking that women would probably beat a path to his door.

It was wonderfully warm inside and she shed her outer layers with alacrity, stripping down to one of his long-sleeved tee-shirts and some of his jogging bottoms.

Then she stood back and looked at him for a few seconds while he stared back at her.

'Spit it out.'

'I beg your pardon?' Alice said.

'You've been acting a little odd all morning. What's bothering you? Is it the fact that you've realised you have no choice but to stay *cooped up here* for another day?'

Alice flushed. 'Sorry, I didn't mean to sound ungrateful. *Cooped up* isn't the right word. I was, yes, just hoping that I might be on my way, so you'll have to excuse me if I'm not my usual self this morning.'

'You barely had any breakfast. You must be hungry.'

'I had more than enough.' Alice drew herself up to her very unimpressive five-three height and sucked in her stomach.

'Right. Well, I suppose we should discuss how the day is going to unfold. More coffee?'

He headed off to the kitchen without waiting for an answer and Alice followed him. In the cold light of day, and freed from the aftermath of her near-death experience on the slopes in a blizzard, she had taken the opportunity to really look at the chalet properly.

It was very, *very* luxurious but in an understated way. There was nothing flash anywhere but she could tell that all the bathroom fittings in her *en suite* were of the highest standard. There was a lot of marble and the towels were the sort that must have cost the earth. And, again, the bedroom was understated luxury. The linen was soft and silky and probably had the highest possible thread-count. The cupboards were made of solid wood and the rug on the ground, like all the rugs in the lodge, was softly faded, with the sheen of pure silk.

The view from the windows was absolutely staggering: vistas of pristine white, a vision of another world uncluttered by houses, people, restaurants, shops or life at all, come to think of it.

Fixing people's computers or designing websites obviously paid big-time.

Looking around the kitchen, she could see that everything in it likewise carried the stamp of quality. She sat and smoothed her hand over the table and watched as he made a pot of coffee.

'So, do you do lots of skiing while you're here? You must be an excellent skier to tackle these slopes. Where did you learn?'

Mateo turned round, carried the coffee to the table and then sat opposite her, angling his chair so that he could extend his legs to the side, crossed at the ankles.

He'd had a restless night. It had never happened before, not here. Here, he could always bank on some solid, battery-recharging down time. But he'd gone to bed thinking of the woman sitting opposite him and wondering why she'd managed to get to him the way she had.

He'd found himself actively looking forward to seeing her this morning—crazy. And, crazier, the fact that she was off for some reason and that, too, was bugging him. It seemed he'd completely forgotten lessons learnt from past experience, from a tough childhood, an even tougher adolescence and a woman who had done a number on him. He just didn't get it. He'd could have given a master class on how to avoid the pitfalls of being vulnerable to anything and anyone…and yet this woman ignited something inside him. Uneasily, he knew that it wasn't just physical.

'I…have experience of these mountains. I learnt to ski here when I was very young. Start young enough, and you become a master before you hit your teens. Same with every sport.' He shrugged and was about to change the subject when she interrupted.

'Agreed. I learnt reasonably young when my class went on a ski trip. I absolutely loved it from the beginning. I just loved the way flying down those slopes made me feel free.'

Momentarily distracted, with a shuttered expression Mateo watched her mobile, expressive heart-shaped face. Her eyes were bright and she was leaning forward, her unruly hair tumbling over her shoulders and her chin propped in one hand. Her natural sunny nature was coming through once again, and it was weird how satisfied that made him feel.

No harm letting the conversation flow, he concluded.

He didn't want her feeling down while she was here. That was simply because it would make for an uncomfortable atmosphere—not because he, personally, liked to see her smile and hear her laugh.

'Free from what?' he probed.

'Oh, you know, the usual stuff… I adore my parents, but I'm an only child, and even though they always made a big point of letting me do my own thing I still always felt them hovering in the background.' She laughed. He noticed her laughter rippled like water over stones. 'You know how parents are—they can be super-protective even when they don't want to be. What about you—are you an only child?'

'I am, as it happens.'

'Then I'll bet you get what I'm talking about.'

'Not entirely.' Mateo flushed darkly as her hazel eyes rested on him, curious but not intrusive, just gently questioning. Then, without thinking, he said in a rough undertone, 'My mother died when I was young—eight. I was raised by my father.'

'Oh, my word, Mateo, I'm so sorry. How awful that must have been for you.'

Mateo instinctively made to pull back as she reached out to him, but then he let his hand rest on the table and let his fingers be squeezed by hers.

'You're very emotional, aren't you?' he said gruffly. 'I'm not a great believer in all this kumbaya nonsense.' But, still, her fingers were warm and the feel of them stirred something in him. He remembered what it had felt like to look after his father, to be that amateur boxer fighting for money, to be working life out on his own. To be on a road no kid should have been on from the age of eight. To know, far too young, that the only person who could save him was himself.

'I'm not emotional, I'm empathetic. It must have been a horrible time for you, and lonely as well. I'm sure your father was wonderful, but sometimes the grief of adults can take over, leaving their kids stranded for a while.'

'I… I admit something like that did occur, but naturally I rose to the occasion and found a way out. It's in the past.' He tugged his hand free but could still feel the warmth of her skin against his. 'Something else I don't do that you can add to your list: I don't dwell. Only reason I mentioned it at all was to say that my experiences as an only child perhaps don't quite dovetail with yours. But, getting back to what we need to discuss: plans for how today is going to unfold.'

'How did you cope? Were there other family members around you to help you deal with the situation?'

'Now you're beginning to sound like a therapist on a mission,' Mateo said wryly. 'For the record, there were no aunts and uncles fretting and clucking. I coped with the situation the way I have always coped with all situations: on my own.'

Alice felt her heart go out to the guy whose face was so unrevealing of the hurt he must have endured as a child. He was so commanding and so tough, yet underneath there surely must be a vulnerability there, a hangover from his childhood experiences?

'It must have been lonely. How long did your dad hide away, Mateo?'

'Whoever said anything about *hiding away*?' He clicked his tongue impatiently but her eyes never left his face. 'A few years,' he expanded. 'He took time off for a few years.'

'And you were left to pick up the pieces all on your own,' Alice murmured softly.

'Setbacks always make a person stronger.'

She didn't say anything. She just continued to gaze at him in silence then she nodded and took a deep breath.

'Of course, you're right: setbacks can make you stronger. So, today…'

He was proud. Taking this conversation any further was going to make him shut down and Alice got the feeling that, once Mateo shut down, he would never open up again. Of course, she wasn't going to be around to have any more deep and meaningful conversations with him about his past, but curiosity about him bit into her with sharp, persistent teeth.

Also, for reasons she couldn't fathom, she didn't want him to turn away from her because she was getting too nosey. She didn't know why it mattered but it did— maybe because they were confined here, so it was best for them to get along. Yes, that was it.

'About today…' Mateo drawled, picking up where she had left off and strolling to the coffee pot on the counter to get a refill. 'I usually catch up on my skiing when I'm here but, considering there's no chance of that, I will spend my time catching up on work instead.'

'Really? You can do that computer stuff remotely?'

'Yes,' Mateo said gently. 'That "computer stuff" can all be done remotely.'

'And I suppose time is money when you're working for yourself.'

'Never a truer word has ever been spoken. I have an office off my suite, so you won't see me for most of the day. Sadly, there's nothing here I can think of to occupy your time, and in the absence of a spare laptop…'

'I can do stuff on my phone. I can plan out lessons

for the remainder of the term. Do you have any paper—pens, perhaps?'

'Paper? Pens?'

Alice burst out laughing. 'Now you're making me think of some of my children at school,' she teased. 'They're experts when it comes to computers, but show them a pen and tell them to write an essay and suddenly I'm asking them to fly to the moon. I teach eleven-year-olds, and my mission is to remind them that the old school way of doing things is still important.'

Mateo grinned. 'Technology makes everything quicker.'

'Which is why it makes our brains lazy. If you can press a button and have all the information you need right there, then how are you ever going to learn the value of research?'

'The "click of the button" scenario leaves time for other important things to be done instead of sifting through old tomes in a library and highlighting sentences and folding pages…'

'Both of which would incur a fine for destruction of public property.' Alice grinned back at him.

'I stand duly corrected.'

Their eyes tangled, the silence stretched and Mateo was the first to break it.

'And to answer your question,' he said gruffly, 'I happen to have both.' He stood up, suddenly keen to escape the confines of the kitchen, which now felt suffocating. One minute he'd been backing away from a personal conversation he hadn't encouraged but seemed to be indulging, and the next minute she was making him laugh.

He was suddenly keen to escape. He needed time-out. He would confine himself to his office and stay put until he got his act together. He left her sitting at the kitchen table and returned five minutes later with a stack of A4 paper and a selection of pens in different colours.

'You use this stuff?'

'The paper, yes. The pens were bought as a standby years ago, just in case the broadband went down and I actually had to…work on some designs manually.'

'Okay.'

'So…er… I'll leave these with you. If you need me, I'll be in my office, but don't count on me for lunch. Help yourself to whatever you want; the fridge is fully stocked. I'll grab something at some point. When I'm working I tend to forget the time.'

'Very bad for you, you know,' she returned absently.

'What's very bad for me?'

'Too much work.'

'Like I said, Alice Reynolds, I play as well as work…'

Alice was forcibly reminded of the evening before, when the conversation between them had felt danger-ously close to the edge…politeness rubbing shoulders with the sort of sexual undertones she wasn't used to but which had electrified her.

She felt as though she'd entered a whole new world. Mateo was so different from any man she had ever come into contact with. He might have a boring job but he certainly was far from boring. He was sophis-ticated, cynical and had the sort of self-assurance that made her tingle all over. But more than that, and more than his stunning looks, there was a sense of complexity about him that had roused her curiosity…and, yes, *turned her on*.

Compared to this beast, Simon was a boy. It was disloyal, but she wondered what she'd seen in him, aside from safety. Just admitting that made her go hot and cold.

'So you mentioned,' she mumbled, thrown back into politeness as words failed her and he burst out laughing.

'Only bores repeat themselves. Am I sensing an insult in there somewhere?'

'No!' Alice reddened and bristled but then grinned sheepishly. 'You're teasing, aren't you?'

'Guilty as charged.'

Mateo appreciated the delicate bloom in her cheeks. He could have added 'teasing' to the list of things he didn't do. But he enjoyed the way she blushed. He'd forgotten what that looked like.

'I'll catch you later,' he muttered. 'If the snow starts to lessen, I'll probably try and do some clearing outside; get it as ready as possible for you to make your escape. There are several rooms towards the back you can use if you want privacy to do whatever you plan on doing…and, like I said, help yourself to whatever you want from the fridge.'

He left before another conversation could commence, luring him in in ways he knew vaguely he shouldn't really like but did.

But work—the thing that always drove him, the one thing that took priority over everything else—proved difficult as the day wore on. By the time he hit the space he used as his office, it was close to lunchtime. He took only a brief break to rustle up a sandwich some time mid-afternoon, with the sun already on its way to setting and the snow still falling thick and fast with no sign of letting up.

Where was Alice?

Having spent hours in front of his computer with very little to show for it, Mateo had a job not hunting her down. His chalet wasn't the biggest in the world but there were nooks and crannies to which she could have retreated, including her suite. He held off knocking on any closed doors but, by the time six rolled round and he'd had a shower and was heading downstairs, he was caught in unusual position of restlessly anticipating something, against his better judgement: *anticipating seeing her.*

She'd lodged in his head and there was no point denying the fact that he *wanted* her. His formidable self-control had deserted him, all because of a woman who just wasn't his type and frankly should have got on his nerves…*sexy as hell or not.* She was as wholesome as apple pie and as sweet as chocolate, and neither of those things were what he looked for in a woman. So what was going on? Was novelty that powerful?

Scowling at a train of thought that refused to go away, Mateo pushed open the kitchen door and then…stopped dead in his tracks. She was there, fridge door open, bending in search of something and offering a sight that made him break out in perspiration. She was in her thermal leggings and they were stretched tight across a peachy rear. The baggy sweater was his but it had ridden up, exposing a sliver of pale skin at her waist.

He was frozen to the spot, and thoughts about why he was so attracted to her were replaced by a series of graphic images that made him feel unsteady. How long had he been standing there staring at her like a horny schoolboy? When she straightened and turned round, he felt as though he'd been caught with his fingers in the till.

Alice hadn't heard him.

How had he managed that? For a guy who was so big, he moved with the stealth of a jungle cat. She blinked, caught completely off-guard. He'd had a shower. His hair was still slightly damp and he was in a pair of faded jeans and a rugby shirt, the sleeves of which he'd shoved up to the elbows.

How long had he been standing in the doorway looking at her?

She frantically tried to think whether she'd made an idiot of herself somehow, bending over to find something to peck on, something sweet and contraband but very much needed after a day of thinking about the guy standing in front of her and feverishly analysing every word they had exchanged.

'I—I...' she stuttered, not moving a muscle. 'I was just...um...looking for something to eat.'

She shut the fridge door but remained where she was as he strolled towards her. With every step closer, her heart beat a little faster, and the blood in her veins felt a little hotter, because there was *something* in that lazy, green gaze that was *hot*.

She licked her lips and stuck her hands behind her back.

'You shouldn't do that,' he ground out shakily.

'Sorry, you said I could help myself to...'

'Not *that*.'

'Then what are you talking about?' Alice raised her eyes to look at him. He was so close that with almost no effort she could reach out and flatten her palm on his chest, and right now there was nothing in the world she would rather do. It was confusing and bewildering, but felt stupidly *right*, as though there was some power-ful electrical connection between them that had sprung from nowhere.

'Bend over like that,' he returned thickly. 'Any red-blooded guy would have trouble resisting...'

'Resisting what?' Just saying those two words felt like the greatest act of daring she had ever undertaken. The challenge of breaking off her engagement faded in comparison. Alice had never been bold like this. She hadn't been raised to ask sexually provocative questions.

A rush of liberating self-discovery flooded her. In not so many words, Mateo had laughed at the concept of a cosy relationship with a boring guy, had laughed at the idea of settling down at the tender of age of twenty-four, and naturally she had bristled in angry response. But this felt good. She was daring to stray from the straight and narrow and it felt great.

'Touching. Want me to spell it out? *Touching*. Because I stood there at the door and saw you bending over and all I wanted to do was touch you.'

He shook his head, raked his fingers through his dark hair and shot her a frustrated look from under his lashes. 'Apologies,' he muttered. 'Forget I said that.'

'Maybe I don't want to,' Alice returned then, stretching recklessness to the point of no return, she did what she'd been itching to do and rested her hand on his chest.

His chest was all muscle under the sweater. She felt faint.

'No?' came a lazy drawl. His hand covered hers. 'Then tell me, Alice Reynolds, what you *do* want…'

'You.'

Had she really said that? Yes, she had, and it was more than liberating…it was empowering!

'I want *you*, Mateo Whatever-your-last-name-might-be!'

'Are you sure, Alice?' This time his voice was utterly serious, giving her time and space to think, to reconsider, to walk away from something she might rashly have suggested. Alice appreciated that more than she could have said and she gave the question the consideration it deserved.

'I'm sure.' She met his eyes steadily, even though her heart was beating madly inside her and every nerve in her body was at breaking point. 'I've never done anything like this before,' she confessed in a staccato rush. 'I guess you could say I've led a sheltered life.'

'I think I'd already deduced that, which why I'm telling you right now that, if you want to walk away from this, then you can. I might have to take several cold showers to calm my erection, but so be it.'

'Erection…' She rolled that sexy word on her tongue and melted.

'Would you like to have a feel of what I'm talking about, Alice Reynolds?'

'You've probably slept with way more experienced women…'

'You mean as the ski-instructor I'm not? You turn me on. And I'm not lying when I say that I can't remember ever being turned on by any woman like this.'

'Really?'

'Too much talking!' He groaned.

He took her hand and guided it to the bulge under his jeans. Alice closed her eyes and just wanted to pass out. She fumbled with the zip, eventually managed to tug it down, then she hooked her fingers into the waistband and daringly lowered the jeans.

She looked down at the black boxers and then circled his erection through the light cotton. It was thick and impressively big. She was so wet for him that her underwear felt irritating and uncomfortable, but the connection felt too strong to break. She was turned on even more by his groan of pleasure as she reached into his boxers to feel the muscle and sinew of his hardness. Raw instinct and driving desire replaced her lack of experience. She began to stroke him in long, regular slow strokes, watching as she touched, wanting to take him in her mouth so that the connection could get even stronger. Wanting *him* to do the same to her, to touch her and take her in his mouth.

'I'm not going to be able to hold off if you keep doing that,' he said hoarsely and then he scooped her up and began walking towards his bedroom. He carried her as though she weighed nothing. It was downright thrilling. He kicked shut the bedroom door behind them and then gently laid her on his bed as though she were a piece of delicate porcelain.

He pressed a remote and the shutters came down on the scene outside of snowy, grey twilight, leaving them in shadow. She was still fully dressed but now she watched as he shed what remained of his clothes, the jumper and the boxers, to stand completely naked in front of her. He was all gorgeous, rampant alpha male and, for tonight, *all hers*—a looming, heart-stopping invitation to untold pleasure.

'Enjoying the view?' He smiled and moved towards her. 'My turn now...'

CHAPTER FOUR

ALICE WONDERED WHERE this passionate side of her had been hiding all her life. Simon had certainly not managed to locate it and yet she had never given that a second's thought; she had simply accepted that love was something calm and controlled.

Maybe it was, she thought now in a muddled way, thrilling to his approach as he settled on the mattress and began the business of *enjoying the view*.

Maybe love was calm and controlled but this thing she felt wasn't love—it was desire.

In hindsight, she might not have loved Simon, although she'd been super-fond of him. She'd certainly never *wanted* him, not like this, not with this feeling of her whole body going up in flames.

Mateo tugged down the lined leggings which she had worn, because she'd known that they'd hardly be visible under his sweater, which almost reached her knees. She was breathing quickly as the leggings were stripped off and she squeezed her eyes tightly shut to block out any rush of self-consciousness at the sight of her pale thighs exposed to his roving gaze.

He was so beautiful and she was so...*nothing to write home about*.

'Don't...' she heard him murmur softly. She opened one eye to look at him and saw that he was smiling.

He abandoned the striptease and moved to lie alongside her, then he manoeuvred her so that they were looking at one another, her breasts pushing against his chest, her bare legs against his.

'Don't what?' she asked, both eyes open now, but shyly.

'Close your eyes. How can you enjoy what I want to do to you if you're not looking at me?'

'You're so beautiful, Mateo.'

He burst out laughing and, when he looked at her next, his gaze was hot and the smile was still lingering there.

'So are you. And you're so refreshing...and sexy... and funny...'

'You're just saying that.'

'Open your eyes and enjoy the way I touch you... like this.'

Alice kept her eyes locked to his as he slipped his hand underneath the crotch of her underwear and wriggled his finger into her wet crease until he found the pulsing bud of her clitoris. She gasped, squirmed and then gripped his shoulders. The thick sweater was an impediment and her breasts felt heavy and sensitive underneath it.

'See how much better that is?' he purred with silky assurance. 'It's even better when we talk...and I don't mean make small talk about the weather; I mean something a little raunchier than that. Maybe we'll leave that for the moment. For the moment…just keep your eyes open. Let me see the expression on your face when I touch you.'

Alice was in a world she'd never known existed. An explosion of desire burst inside her like a firecracker and she fumbled, tugged and unclasped until not only the cloying sweater had been removed, but the vest and bra underneath. Her eyes were very much wide open as she took in his rampant, masculine appreciation at the sight of her breasts.

It was an out-of-body experience, something she had never imagined possible. She was no longer Alice Reynolds who had always stuck to the straight and narrow, and in whom principles of what was and wasn't expected had been embedded. She'd burst through those barriers into a whole different world and was, just for now, just in this instant, a reckless, wanton woman with needs that shocked her.

She groaned, writhed and kept looking as he straddled her and sank to explore her breasts with his hands, mouth and tongue. He took an engorged nipple into his mouth and tugged the straining bud until she was on the point of coming even though his fingers were no longer teasing her down there.

It was so erotic, so exquisite. There was no room for inhibitions of any kind as he suckled on her nipples and then explored further, licking a delicate trail down her stomach and finding the place he had found with his finger but this time with his tongue. The intimacy of it made her want to squeeze her legs shut but he parted her thighs and, when he began to lick her, she had to stifle the guttural cries of pleasure that wanted to find a way out of her.

The rise of passion bursting its banks was unstoppable and she spasmed against his exploring mouth, her whole body shuddering and arching. Her mind went completely blank and, when the final quivers subsided, their eyes met and he gave a satisfied smile. He fumbled to find his wallet and produced a condom, which made her think vaguely that this was a guy who took no chances.

Her body was still throbbing, gearing up for that final, deep satisfaction that would come from feeling him inside her, and she parted her legs and opened up to him with eagerness and rising desire.

He thrust into her and a reservoir of pleasure she hadn't even known she'd been holding back raced through her and she came again, her rhythm matching his, their bodies perfectly tuned, reaching orgasm at the same time.

It was joyful…earth-shattering and glorious. If she'd thought that the reckless, wanton woman would go back into hiding when the sex was over, then she'd been wrong. The door he'd unlocked was still wide open as he settled next to her, his arm shielding his face as his body began to unwind. She curved against him and gently rested her hand on his chest.

'How was that?' he murmured.

'Very nice, thank you.'

'And to think that I was looking for a more exuberant response.'

But there was laughter in his voice and she smiled against him. 'Is it always like that for you?' Alice murmured drowsily.

'It's been known. Want to have a shower? Head down with me so that something can be done about dinner?'

'I'd completely forgotten about that.'

'Sex does that to a person. Makes you forget what's happening out there in the big, bad world.'

That made Alice think of the big, bad world he referred to, otherwise known as *reality*. She would be back in school in a matter of days. She hadn't phoned her parents, but she would, just as soon as she returned home. Their gentle questioning and eager interest in how her holiday had gone would be a timely reminder that what she was enjoying now was very far removed from her day-to-day life. This flare of attraction had hit them both like a ton of bricks but it wouldn't do to forget that it had only happened because they were stuck here in his lodge, snowbound.

Would their paths ever have crossed otherwise? Not in a month of Sundays. Forget about how different their backgrounds were—they just weren't compatible on any level. She might have taken time-out here from the person she really was but that person would be back in just over a week: cheerful, dependable, easy going... and still looking for the guy of her dreams, who might not be Simon, but certainly could never be someone like this man who had made her body sing.

She would still want a guy who was dependable and steady, the sort of guy that Mateo might find boring, but who would be the guy who would stand by her through the years until they were old and surrounded by kids and grandchildren. She would still want *normal* but with a guy she adored rather than a guy she was fond of. *Normal* would still be the desired goal.

There was a reason people made such a big deal about the differences between love and lust: one was for ever and the other was for five minutes.

'Want to shower with me?' He broke through her thoughts, his voice low, husky and sexy.

'Really?'

'Never done that before?'

'Not as such.'

Mateo laughed. 'What does *not as such* mean? You took your clothes off, tested the water and then told that guy you dumped that it wasn't the right temperature, maybe another time?'

'Very funny.'

'You're very sweet, Alice.'

'Is that a good thing?'

'It's an unusual thing, at least in my world. In my world, the women aren't sweet.'

'What are they?'

'They're...experienced. Blushing—which you do so well, might I add—is something they left behind before they hit thirteen. You're an only child... Where did you grow up—in London? What do your parents do?'

Alice hesitated. For the first time the thought of admitting that her dad was a vicar felt somehow a little embarrassing. She'd had a pretty idyllic childhood all told, but to this worldly guy, who dated experienced women and had had a tragic background, her relatively uncomplicated life might seem a bit dreary.

She laughed at herself for being silly.

'Well, I was born in a tiny village in Wales, but my family moved to Surrey when I was still quite young.'

'Quite a culture shock I'd imagine. Did you have relatives there? Did your father get a job transfer?'

'You could say it was a job transfer, yes...' She sighed and looked at him a little sheepishly. 'My dad's a vicar, you see.'

'Your dad's *a vicar*?'

'There's no need to sound quite so shocked,' Alice said defensively. 'Lots of people are vicars!'

He stared at her. In the darkness, she could make out the glitter of his eyes and the shadowy angles of his beautiful face. What was he thinking?

'Makes sense.' His voice was neutral and his eyes were serious. 'There's an innocence to you.' It was his turn to sigh. 'This was a mistake.'

'What?'

'This...us...making love: a mistake.'

'Please don't say that,' Alice whispered. 'Didn't you enjoy it?'

'Of course I did. But, Alice, like I said, I date women with experience, women who know the score when they sleep with me, and by that I mean women who understand that I'm not in it for the long term. They have no illusions. They're not looking for any happy-ever-afters with me. I suppose I should have made that clear at some point before we hit the bedroom but...'

'Why? Why would you have wanted to make that clear?'

Alice forced a laugh, only to find it turning into a genuine one. Hadn't she just been thinking that she could never fall for a guy like Mateo? Weren't they on the same page, neither interested in anything but living in the moment? She didn't regret what they had just done, even though she knew that maybe she should. Or at least maybe she should ask herself searching questions about how she could have jettisoned the part of her that took the sanctity of relationships as given without any thought at all.

She had never imagined that the only guy she dated would be the one she married, even though it had almost turned out that way; but she *had* always believed that a person didn't just hop in the sack because they happened to be attracted to someone. She *had* always believed that relationships had to mean something.

'Look,' she said firmly. 'I know what this is all about. It's about sex. We're attracted to one another, but there are no strings attached, and I'm not going to be looking for anything once the snow melts and I get out of here.' She met his brooding gaze and grinned. 'You're *so* egotistical.'

'What are you talking about?' he said, frowning.

'You're good-looking and you've been spoiled. You feel you've got to give women a bracing talk on not getting over-involved because you're a commitment-phobe. You think that *every* person you sleep with is out for more than you're prepared to give! You'll just have to accept that I'm not one of them.'

'You *are* nothing like anyone I've ever dated,' he

agreed, gently pushing her hair back and then letting his hand cup her face.

'I don't want anything from you.'

'And I like that.'

'I certainly would never be interested in any guy who was a commitment-phobe.'

'Wise game-plan.'

'Can I ask why, though?'

Mateo looked at her. She was so fresh-faced and, just for a second, he was tempted to spill out his life story. The temptation came as a shock. He felt as though he was being sucked down into something over which he had no control, a rabbit hole. Some crazy place where he was tempted to let go and see what happened next.

It was enough for him abruptly to step back. Control had got him where he was in life. He had controlled his time, his energies and his focused climb to the top. He had lived through the sadness and despair that had ruined his father when he had lost the love of his life. From his own place of quiet grief—with no one to turn to, because it had felt as though his father had been taken from him along with his mother—he had learned the value of never handing control of his life to someone else.

His love life, after the horror story of Bianca, had been even more controlled, if anything, and after she had showed up asking for money years after their divorce nothing in his life had been left up to chance.

The fact that he had already played fast and loose by allowing his physical attraction to the woman staring at him now to dictate his behaviour was an uncomfortable fact. He had no intention of compounding his lapse by launching into a self-indulgent revisiting of his past or contemplating rabbit holes full of unknown outcomes.

'You can go right ahead and ask.' He tempered the coolness of his voice with a smile. 'But I'll be sticking to "no comment" on that one. And, now that we've had this illuminating conversation, can I entice the sexy vicar's daughter into a little more mutual physical exploration, or will it be shower and something to eat…?'

'Food beckons,' Alice murmured drowsily.

'Agreed.' Mateo's voice was laced with amusement. 'It's important to have stamina when it comes to the business of making love…'

The driving force of the snow eased off but somehow it was agreed that two nights together would become two more.

'Why not?' They'd been in bed at one-thirty in the afternoon, lazy and content after making love, and Mateo's voice had been soft and persuasive. 'We haven't exhausted the passion between us yet, have we? I certainly haven't. I haven't even been tempted to go out there and put the skis on, which is a first for me. So phone your friends and tell them that the kindly family who rescued you from the blizzard want you to stay on until they leave.'

'I'm not sure I mentioned anything about a kindly family,' Alice had returned drowsily, but her mind had already been racing ahead, eagerly accepting his proposition and mothballing the little voice inside her warning her that she was playing with fire.

It had only been a couple of days but he had cast a spell over her. She'd never met anyone like him. She still didn't know that much about him, aside from the skeleton list of facts he had given her in passing, but she didn't care, because what she *did* know was that he was clever, thoughtful, witty and mind-blowingly sexy.

Could stolen time feel more glorious?

She'd made a something and nothing excuse about staying on to her friends, which might have been a little problem, given her limited amount of clothing, but that hadn't mattered because lots of the time was spent without any on at all.

'I'll make it up to you,' she had told Bea on the phone the day before. 'It's so rude, and I know we'd all banked on spending time together, but…'

But she'd discovered a selfish streak in herself and she just hadn't been able to face the prospect of saying goodbye to Mateo. Not yet, not when she didn't have to. And what was so wrong with grabbing this little window of fun and stepping out of her predictable comfort zone? That comfort zone would be waiting for her when she returned to London.

'I just feel that to ski back for the sake of a day before we all leave, well, it feels more recuperative to… er…stay put and recover from my ordeal.'

And she would have another two fantastic days here with Mateo… She was being selfish but it had felt like taking charge of her decision making.

And today they would ski to the little town he had mentioned when she had first landed on his doorstep so that she could replenish her wardrobe. It all felt very clandestine and exciting.

Taking the stairs at a quick trot, she stopped and just gazed at Mateo, who was scrolling on his phone by the door, all black ski gear, his ski sunglasses on his forehead. He was all sexy, gorgeous male.

Not for a second did she regret staying on.

He glanced up at her and smiled slowly.

He'd surprised himself by giving in to impulse and asking her to stay with him for the rest of the time he was at the lodge. Having spent years valuing the sanity and solitude he got here, he'd done a complete about-turn.

She'd said yes, and he'd found that he'd been holding his breath, desperate for her to concur.

'We could always drive. The snow stopped yesterday and the roads down to the town will be passable. No need to take to the slopes.'

He was talking, but mostly relishing the sight of her as she walked towards him. Her ski outfit hugged womanly curves that were still managing to keep him in a state of semi-permanent arousal. She'd tied her hair back and stuffed it into a colourful woolly hat, but tendrils had already escaped, and his fingers itched to twirl one of them round his fingers.

Frankly, he itched to do a hell of a lot more than that. He itched to release the weight of her heavy breasts straining against her stretchy top, to feel them in his hands, to lathe the big, blushing pink nipples with his tongue and mouth, to feel her responsive wetness between her thighs and hear her little cries when he touched her there.

'If we leave now...' he banished those pleasantly erotic images to savour when he could do something about them '...we can be there in twenty minutes and back here within a couple of hours. Lunch at one of the cafés might be nice.'

'We should take a backpack for whatever I buy.'

'Already thought of that. Let's go; if we stay here much longer, I'm going to have to put this little trip on hold and take you back to bed.'

Alice laughed and told him they should take to the slopes and not go by car.

He was a brilliant skier. The conditions were now perfect for skiing: light, steady snow overnight had led to a cushioned, pillowy path down, with just enough grip for her to handle the challenging turns. He kept pace with her and she knew that he was slowing himself down. She was experienced but he took experience to a new level.

They made it to the town in under half an hour and it was as bustling and charming as she had expected, with shops—expensive boutiques catering for the expensive tourist.

Alice had tried to stop him from shopping with her but he'd raised his eyebrows and insisted on accompanying her into the shops. All seven of them, from what he could count.

'You'll be bored,' she'd warned.

'I never get bored looking at you. You could do a few

twirls for me. I like the thought of that. I could sit and admire the view whilst smoking a cigar.'

'You don't smoke.'

'True.'

Now, looking at her from under his lashes, Mateo knew exactly what was going through her head: the price of the things she was rifling through. The places here were all exclusive. The salespeople all resembled models and the shops were achingly modern and austere with the clothes arranged artfully on mannequins without heads.

'Let me get this.' He wasn't sure whether this was the right thing to suggest or not, but the embarrassed hesitation on her face and the way she couldn't quite meet his eyes stirred something fiercely protective in him.

'Don't be ridiculous!'

'I persuaded you to stay. If it weren't for me, you'd be back at your chalet with your friends and a suitcase full of clothes you'd brought with you.'

'There's no way I would accept anything from you, Mateo. I know you earn more than me; I'm not blind. But you're still self-employed and I know what that means. You could be earning good money now but you never know what's round the corner.'

'My corners are pretty predictable.'

'I still don't want you getting me anything,' she told him quietly. 'I can't afford much, but I don't need much, and I've already eaten you out of house and home.'

He'd watched as she'd turned away and chosen the cheapest jumper on show and the cheapest waterproof trousers, along with one pair of grey jogging bottoms. It was such a novel experience, not paying for whatever a woman wanted, that he wasn't sure whether to feel terrible or oddly pleased.

Or deceitful, considering she was oblivious to how much he was worth. He ruled the last out because he wasn't deceiving her. He was simply living in the moment with a woman who was likewise doing the same. Within this scenario, what he earned or didn't earn was irrelevant.

'In that case,' he said, shopping concluded as they stood outside, both of them briefly admiring the quaint buildings and the pretty tree-lined streets, 'I insist on buying lunch. Like you said, I have more than you.'

He'd wanted to do more. He'd wanted to take her into some more shops, buy stuff for her, but knew better than to go near that suggestion.

A couple of hours later, they were back at his lodge, and he smiled wolfishly at her. 'Okay, you denied me the masculine pleasure of treating you to whatever you wanted...'

'I'm very independent like that.' Alice laughed, standing on tiptoe to kiss him.

'Didn't you let your fiancé buy things for you?'

Mateo stripped off, dumping outer garments on hooks and ski boots on the ground, watching her as he did so.

'That's different, and anyway, there wasn't much money flying around for unnecessary purchases.'

'So that's "he didn't treat me to little surprise gifts because he was thoughtless"...'

Alice burst out laughing, her eyes warm and alight. 'You bought lunch. I'll cook for you in return.' She looked at him, her expression trusting and open, a smile still playing on her lips. 'Or, at any rate, I'll give it a go.'

Mateo stilled. He had never done domesticity. He and Bianca had gone out, socialising with the glamorous crew that tagged along in the wake of successful sportsmen, and he had been a very successful amateur boxer with his admiring followers. But cosy nights in had been few and far between. Bianca had loathed cooking. They'd eaten out most nights, or else had takeaways, and in fairness he'd been living with his father when he'd been dating her. And post marriage they'd rented a place, but somehow the business of cooking for one another, watching telly and discussing long term plans had never materialised. They hadn't had that sort of relationship. She'd wanted to socialise, and had wanted the thrill of being admired. There had been no room for domesticity in that scenario and that was just the way he'd liked it.

Buried deep inside him were too many memories of what that domesticity had felt like once upon a time, when he'd been a kid and the house had smelled of cooking and rang to the sound of laughter and love. His parents had been so in love. Domesticity, he'd decided a long time ago, was the flashpoint where want became need, and need became the sort of vulnerability that could be your undoing.

Mateo had always made sure that women didn't get their feet under the table. That was always going to be the safe route. He could handle the woman who wanted glamour and the thrill of being envied and admired by other men. He could handle the women who were like his ex, because they were a known quantity. He liked it that way and the women he dated liked it that way as well. They enjoyed being treated to the very best money could offer and, as someone accustomed to being a loner, he was content with that. Enjoyment without emotional involvement: standard procedure.

He'd done the cooking since Alice had arrived, which was fair enough: his house, his food, his responsibility. But now, just like that, he realised how much he had confided in her, how much of himself he had exposed.

Suddenly he was gripped by an uneasy claustrophobia. Alice was chatting, moving to the fridge and whipping out stuff to make a meal. In the space of only a few days, she knew the layout of this kitchen as well as he did. Hell, when had that happened?

'Like I said, things were different with Simon,' she was saying. 'Although, in fairness, we pooled our finances. He wasn't thoughtless, although... Hmm; where do you keep the chopping boards, Mateo? I'm not up to your standard but I can produce something edible from what we've got in the fridge.'

'Alice...'

His voice was raw and he shifted uncomfortably, raking his fingers through his hair, not knowing what to do or what exactly to say, just knowing that he felt threatened, that somehow he had to escape.

She did things to him, stirred things inside him, and he didn't want that. He didn't need it. He wasn't going to start flinging doors open that led to places he'd spent his life protecting.

* * *

Alice knew from the driven urgency of his voice that whatever was on the tip of his tongue was going to be something she didn't want to hear.

'You'd rather cook yourself.' She laughed nervously. She knew what this was about; of course she did. She could see it on his face. He'd warned her off and she'd... She only gone and developed feelings for him; only forgotten that this was time-out and that he was a guy who didn't want her around once they left this bubble.

She felt tears sting the back of her eyes. How could this have happened? She'd thought herself so sorted when it came to what kind of guys she wanted in her life. Had the very nature of her background played a part in what had happened in this hideaway? Had she been so sheltered and so cosseted that she had never developed the truly tough streak that could guide her when it came to men? Surely, if that were the case, then this wouldn't feel so *right*? If that were the case, then this would feel like lust, instead of which it felt like...

She lowered her eyes and breathed in deeply, then she looked at him without flinching.

'This is beginning to bore you, isn't it?' she said quietly.

'This is beginning to...become too complicated.'

'Why?'

'Do I need to have a reason?'

'No.' She could feel her heart hammering inside her and her limbs were turning to jelly.

'You deserve a reason,' he said roughly.

'I guess by "complications" you mean you think I'm getting too attached.'

'Aren't you?'

'Because I offered to cook a meal for us?' Alice cried, hands on her hips as she glared at him.

Dismay and downright terror at the thought that she really had serious feelings—*loved him, even*—made her fight back. He didn't want her. He might still *desire* her, but he no longer *wanted* her around. They were getting a little too comfortable with one another. Alice steadied her breath. What was wrong with getting comfortable with someone? Teetering on a tightrope of confusion and indecision, she took the plunge. Being open, honest and truthful was always the right way to be. She'd been taught that. It was embedded in her DNA.

'We get along,' she said with driving sincerity. 'Don't we? Or am imagining that?'

'I never said we didn't.'

'And the sex is great, terrific…the best. At least for me, and you seemed to enjoy the times we spent in bed making love.'

'Again, ditto.'

'Then why are you so scared that this is complicated? It's straightforward, Mateo.'

'Alice, you don't get it.'

'What we have could be something really good, really special! Don't you feel that as well? I mean, I'm not saying that we're going to end up walking down the aisle together or anything…' She laughed nervously again but actually, in her head, she was toying with the seductive notion of this beautiful man asking her to marry him.

Her heart fluttered. 'But we could do it justice by see-ing where it leads, don't you think?'

'Alice, I was married once before.'

Alice opened her mouth, closed it and stared at him in utter shock. The thought that he might have been married hit her like a bolt from the blue. She shuffled over to one of the chairs by the table, flopped into it and continued staring at him, open-mouthed.

'What happened?'

'What happened was a divorce,' Mateo ground out, 'after a short, unfortunate time together.'

'I… I'm so sorry. You never said.'

'Is there any reason why I should have? Alice, I told you that I wasn't interested in anything beyond what we have here and now.'

'I know.'

'I'm not looking for a relationship. I had one of those and I will never repeat the mistake.'

'But what about love?'

'Not for me. In time, when singledom becomes a place I no longer wish to inhabit, then I'll consider set-tling down with a woman like me—a woman who sees the practical side to a relationship and isn't looking for a fairy-tale romance. A companion, in other words, who is as practical as I am when it comes to the concept of marriage, or at least cohabitation.'

Their eyes met. What else was there to say? Alice was comfortable with what she'd done and, if inwardly he sneered at her for speaking what was on her mind, then so be it. Once she left here, she would never set eyes on him again, but at least she would leave with her conscience intact and no regrets about letting pride stand in the way of truth.

And at least she hadn't made a complete fool of herself by going the distance and actually confessing just how deeply ran her feelings for him.

'Well,' she said with a tight smile, 'just for the record, it's been fun. My mistake for thinking we could have a little more fun when we got to London. I'll go get my stuff together and I'll be out of your hair.'

'It'll be dark in an hour. You know you're welcome to stay here for the night.'

'You've seen how experienced a skier I am and the snow is good. I can make it back to my side of the mountain. The girls have gone, but it'll be easy to rent somewhere for the night, and I can change my ticket by paying a fee.'

She didn't give him the chance to prolong the conversation. She spun round on her heels and walked away.

Mateo watched her leave the kitchen. His stomach was knotted. Of course, this was the right thing. He'd taken his eye off the ball and allowed things to get out of hand. She wasn't like him. She lacked the experience to put things in perspective.

He thought about that soft, sexy body and sweet, sexy personality and tightened his jaw. The truth was that this was good for her. He didn't want to hurt her and she'd be hurt if she stuck around, if they continued this when they returned to London.

Reality had no room for it—not *his* reality. He couldn't love, wasn't interested in it, and it was always going to be better this way. He was never going to go down rabbit holes, so it was sensible to back away from their dubious, treacherous allure. So yes, maybe he'd felt something for her, maybe he'd had a moment of weakness because she'd caught him by surprise, because she was so different from his ex and every single woman who had come after his ex. But happiness was an illusion and he was way too cynical to trade in illusions.

He headed back out, back to the town. He'd get the cable up later when he knew she was gone.

CHAPTER FIVE

SITTING BEHIND HIS DESK in the impressive glass tower that dominated the London skyline, Mateo was in a state of shock. It was over six weeks since Alice Reynolds had disappeared from his life. He could recall that final conversation as vividly as if it had taken place five minutes before.

She had wanted more. She had wanted to continue their relationship when they returned to London. It had been a simple enough suggestion. As she'd told him, bemused and just a little bit pleading, *they got along, didn't they? And the sex was great, wasn't it?* She'd seen it through the straightforward eyes of someone whose life had never been complicated. Her back story hadn't left her cynical, her emotions sealed behind doors that would never be opened.

Yes, she'd left a broken engagement behind her, but it had been obvious from everything she'd said that the solid security of her very loving and protected background had fortified her against any bitterness that the broken engagement might have generated. She hadn't left her heart behind along with the engagement ring.

She'd kept her dreams intact, emulating her parents, he expected.

It had been too much for him. He'd had to walk away. He might have given her the speech about not wanting commitment, but the minute he'd seen her pottering in his kitchen, comfortable in the role of his partner, he'd realised that those warning words had fallen on deaf ears. Even if she herself hadn't realised it, she'd been well on the way to *wanting more*.

Torn between desperately wanting her to stay and knowing she should leave, he had headed back down to the town and, when he'd returned, she was no longer there. She'd airbrushed herself out of his life and, typically, he'd reacted by spending the night in the loving arms of some excellent red wine.

In the morning he'd woken groggily to the realisation that there was no way he was going to hang around a minute longer in the lodge and he'd left for London on the first flight back.

That episode in his life was over. Okay, so there hadn't been a single day when she hadn't crossed his mind, and sure, his attempts at distraction with another woman—a six-foot-tall raven-haired model with a figure that had men walking into lampposts—had flamboyantly failed, but that was because what he and Alice had had had come to a premature end.

It was no surprise that his thoughts were still wrapped up with her because his nose had been put out of joint. He was so accustomed to calling the shots and ending things when his levels of boredom had been reached that to find himself on the receiving end naturally had left a few lingering remnants of bitter aftertaste. It wouldn't last, and indeed it was quite amusing, really. It seemed his ego was bigger than he thought.

So fifteen minutes ago, when his PA had buzzed through to tell him that an Alice Reynolds was in the foyer requesting a meeting, he'd been gobsmacked.

And satisfied; he couldn't help himself. Now, relaxing back in his chair with the busy streets of London sprawling twelve storeys below, visible through the massive sheet of floor-to-ceiling glass, Mateo savoured the taste of what was to come. She'd found out who he was. He had no idea how, but in this day and age sleuthing was easy. Maybe he'd left some form of identification lying around somewhere and she'd seen his full name.

It was disappointing that she'd decided to turn up, because he'd really thought that she lacked that materialistic streak that might let her see the financial benefits of dating a rich guy. She'd struck him as pure as the driven snow, the type of girl who really fitted the bill when it came to being a vicar's daughter.

But he couldn't be right all the time. She was here. She wanted to reconnect some way because he was a catch.

He would have to gently let her down. But he would also have a chance to *see* her and he couldn't deny that that was an exciting prospect.

There was a good chance that his mind had been playing tricks on him for the past few weeks and that the woman who had driven him crazy with desire would not be what he remembered in the cold light of day...

* * *

Alice was told to wait by a glamorous blonde woman, one of several receptionists manning the impressive granite desk in the foyer of the building.

She'd taken the morning off work, determined to be at Mateo's work place as early as possible to get the whole business out of the way.

She'd braced herself for what she was going to say, and had been reasonably calm on the Tube getting here, but now that she was actually *here* she could feel nerves tightening her stomach into knots. There was a buzzing in her ears that was making her feel faint. It was a while since she had seen Mateo. She'd laid her cards on the table, been knocked back and had made her way back to London, never expecting to set eyes on him again.

She winced every single time she thought of the night she'd spent crying in the tiny room she'd rented before taking the next flight out on her altered ticket. She'd left his lodge crying, had returned to London crying and, in between her tears, her misery and having to put on a brave face because she was back at work, it had never occurred to her that there might be anything else to worry about aside from a broken heart.

She hadn't noticed missing her period. They were a law unto themselves, anyway, so there had been no warning signal that something might be up until her boobs had started feeling sore and she had spent mornings feeling queasy.

Then, without really believing anything could possibly be amiss, she had taken a test. Sitting on a toilet seat in the staff bathroom at school, she had watched the stick foretell the vast change in life plan heading her way.

She was pregnant.

How? How on earth had it happened? He'd been careful, hadn't he? There had been a couple of occasions, during sleepy early-morning sex, when maybe he hadn't been able to resist entering her. But he'd remedied that, hadn't he? He had fetched protection in time, hadn't he?

She'd racked her brains, thinking back, but had barely been able to focus because her mind was far too occupied with the life developing inside her: a baby she hadn't planned but a baby she wanted with all her heart.

Every maternal urge in her had kicked in the minute that little stick had given her the unexpected news. All life was precious and this baby inside her would be welcomed into the world with all the fanfare he or she deserved, even if there would be no proud father at the birth.

She would tell Mateo. There had been no hesitation in accepting that, even though the prospect of breaking the news to him filled her with dread. It had occurred to her that he hadn't wanted to continue anything with her to the extent that he'd made sure not to tell her his surname, but in fact she'd had no trouble finding out who he was. She'd simply phoned one of the ski-instructors she knew and asked if he knew who lived in that particular lodge on that part of the mountain.

Ski-instructors were a tightly knit group and Alice had kept in touch with a number of them. And, of course, everyone knew who had classy chalets on the slopes.

Mateo Ricci.

Lost in her thoughts, she came to when a middle-aged lady appeared from nowhere, looked at her with measured curiosity and told her to follow her. Alice wasn't surprised at the overwhelming and impressive surroundings: glass, marble, granite and huge plants artfully dotted around the sweeping foyer.

The minute she had found out Mateo's name, she had looked him up, and *that* was when she'd been surprised, because he wasn't the reasonably successful, freelance computer guy he had made himself out to be. He was the king of the jungle. He didn't work at the beck and call of paymasters—he *was* the paymaster. There were pages and pages of information on him, all relating to his meteoric business rise.

She'd skipped most of it. The one thing she'd taken away was yet more confirmation that she'd been nothing more to him than a few days of fun. She'd been bowled over. He'd been casual. He would have women queuing up for him, but he'd been there and she'd been there, there had been no queues outside his door at that particular point in time…so why not have some fun with the girl who'd been so enthusiastic?

She'd clicked on a lot of images of the sort of women he went out with and, as expected, none of them were built in her mould. He'd found her an amusing novelty toy, because the women he dated were models with legs up to their armpits, the sort of woman Alice would never look like no matter what she did.

She stopped abruptly when the woman in front of her swerved through a smoky glass door and stepped aside to let her pass, and then she was there, in the inner sanctum of the man who had stolen her heart. Even the air seemed more rarefied.

'He's a very busy man.' The lady smiled politely at her.

'I won't be long,' Alice promised. She drew in a deep breath and felt faint as the connecting door to his office was pushed open.

Mateo had moved to stand by the window as he'd waited for her. Now, as he heard the silent whoosh of the connecting door being pushed open, he slowly turned and there she was—hovering in the doorway, then stepping hesitantly into his massive office so that Julie could close the door behind her. She looked like a rabbit caught in the headlights, even though she was obviously trying her best to appear controlled.

She hadn't changed. Mateo's lips thinned with irritation as he felt the abrupt rise in his libido. Hooded eyes drifted down the incredibly drab outfit she had chosen to wear: black, thick cable-knit jumper, jeans, trainers and a bulky waterproof which was slung over her arm. If she had come with the intention of reconnecting with him, then she certainly hadn't pushed the boat out in her attempts to seduce. It should have been a turn-off but was the opposite, much to his annoyance.

He hadn't expected her to have the same effect on him as she'd had when they'd been snowbound in his lodge. He'd concluded that circumstances had contributed to his uncharacteristic out-of-control horniness, but here she was, not saying a word, and the horniness was still there and still out of control, drab clothing or no drab clothing.

'This is an unexpected pleasure.' He swerved round back to his chair behind the conference-table-sized desk and relaxed back, nodding to one of the leather chairs positioned in front.

'I suppose you're surprised to see me here?'

'I'm surprised you found me. How did you achieve that? Did you come across something in the lodge that had my name on it?'

She'd shuffled into the chair he'd indicated and carefully put her coat and backpack on the ground next to her. He realised that he'd forgotten how sexy she was. No wonder the raven-haired model hadn't been able to pass muster. It was because the small, voluptuous siren sitting in front of him still managed to occupy his head.

Who'd have thought that a fling prematurely ended could have such sway over him still? Who could have thought that reason and common sense would count for nothing in the face of a libido he hadn't been able to subdue? It was ridiculous, incomprehensible.

'No, I didn't. I would never have gone nosing around through your personal stuff to find out who you were.'

'But you were obviously still curious enough to find out by some other means, so I'm not that impressed, if I'm honest. But apologies; I'm being rude. Would you like something to drink? Tea? Coffee?'

'I…no. I'm fine, thank you.'

'So you were telling me how you managed to find me.'

'I… I asked around when I got back to London.'

'Enterprising.'

'Do you have to be so sarcastic, Mateo?'

'What were you expecting, Alice? An effusive welcome? The red carpet rolled out? Have you forgotten that what we had no longer exists?' His body was singing from a different song sheet, unfortunately, not nearly so cool as that particular statement. It might be true but what his body wanted was a continuation of what they'd had.

What if she offered to resume their fling and pick up where things had been left off? He felt himself harden at the thought of that gloriously sexy body, so soft and responsive to his touch. He remembered far too vividly for his liking the soft, sweet little noises she made when he caressed her, licked her and explored every inch of her.

His original plan to turn her down flatly and politely when she inevitably offered herself back to him began to fray a little round the edges. The best bet, he decided as pride swooped in to replace hesitation, would be to send her on her way as fast as possible.

For starters, it wouldn't pay to forget why he had decided to finish what they'd enjoyed: she risked being hurt. He had nothing to give and she wanted a lot, too much. He'd warned her and she hadn't listened. Their bubble had burst and that was a good thing.

That said…didn't the fact that she'd showed up here because she'd found out that he was wealthy put paid to his woolly ideas that she was somehow too sweet, too gentle, just too damned *nice* to risk getting wrapped up with a hard-edged guy like him?

'Who did you ask around to get the information?' He reverted to the original topic because he was curious to find out to what lengths she had gone to track him down.

'Remember I told you that I used to teach skiing to beginners on the mountain? I still know loads of the ski-instructors there and also the ones who've left and moved on. They knew who you were.'

'And now you've showed up because…no, let me guess. Having found out that I'm not the freelance tech guy you thought I was, but instead the guy who *owns* those freelance tech guys—and that's just the tip of the iceberg—you decided that it might be worthwhile to explore your options?'

'Explore my options?'

'Dump the innocent act, Alice. There's no need. In fact, if you come clean and admit you've come here to see if what we had can be resurrected, then a conversation is there to be had.' Why kid himself that he still didn't want her? It beggared belief but no amount of burst bubbles, warning talks being ignored about the best option being to send her packing could stifle the insistent pulse of his suddenly reawakened libido.

'You're truly the most cynical person I've ever met in my life, Mateo.'

'I find that's a trait that's always worked in my favour. Give people the benefit of the doubt, and invariably they let you down. So, okay, you're here. You know I have money, and a lot of it, and you want to reconnect. I admit, much as it's frustrating to say so, that I'm tempted by the proposition.'

Their eyes met.

Alice felt the race of her pulse, the hot pumping of blood in her veins. She'd dreaded this meeting and it was turning out that she'd dreaded it for good reason.

He couldn't even be bothered to be polite. The warm, funny, sexy guy she'd fallen for when they'd been locked in by snow was now a stranger in hand-made shoes and a crisp white shirt, sleeves rolled to the elbows, with an expensive barely there logo on the front pocket.

A stranger who thought that she was a gold-digger. And yet, she had to reluctantly concede that she could see where he was coming from. Women chased men with lots of money. Throw looks and charm into the mix, and the combination would certainly attract gold-diggers in a million different guises.

No wonder he'd been livid when she'd turned up at his door! That lodge was probably one of the few completely private getaways he possessed, where no one was around to pester him because no one could physically get there.

But surely *he knew her*?

Yet she'd managed to find him and there could only be one reason for that: that would be the conclusion running through his head.

Alice looked at him from under her lashes with a hint of impatience. She wished she could be angrier at his response but there was something so predictable, so *human*, in his defensiveness, something so weirdly vulnerable in his immediately jumping to that cynical conclusion, that she felt herself soften.

'You're tempted by the proposition, are you?' she queried wryly, allowing him to continue on his tangent just a little bit longer.

'I admit, I've been thinking of you.'

'Have you? I'm surprised.'

'You're incredibly sexy. I reckoned that it might have been the circumstances—the two of us trapped for days in my lodge. I don't have much time for romance, but I'd say that was pretty romantic. I assumed, actually, that that was why I couldn't quite manage to forget about it...us...*you*. That and the fact that it ended before it had run its course.'

'Hmm.'

'I thought,' he continued with searing honesty, 'that I might have been looking back to those few days through rose-tinted specs but the minute I saw you again... You're as sexy as I remembered.'

'I don't know what to say.'

'You don't have to say anything at the moment. You can let me do the talking.'

'Hmm.'

'I still want you and, if you've come here because you think I'm a good bet, then I get that. You wouldn't be the first to be attracted to me because of my bank balance and you won't be the last.'

'That's a very sad statement, Mateo.'

'What are you taking about?'

'Assuming that your bank balance plays a part in why a woman would want to go out with you.'

He spread his arms expansively. 'I'm a realist. You know that. And I'm not too proud to admit that I still want you. The weeks haven't changed that.'

He lowered his voice ominously. 'Although, the rules remain the same. I'm not up for anything but fun, be that fun for days or weeks. And, while we're having fun, the world will be your oyster. Whatever you want, you can have, no expense spared. Diamonds, pearls and sapphires, cars and clothes… You'll find that I'm a generous guy.'

'Diamonds, pearls and sapphires,' Alice murmured. 'What dazzling temptation.'

'Am I missing something here?' He frowned and Alice didn't say anything. She just met his frowning gaze steadily.

'I haven't come here to try and reconnect with you, Mateo. Believe it or not, I'm not the type of person who finds out someone's worth and then decides that they're worth cultivating.'

'I don't understand.'

'I've come here…'

'You maybe want me to donate something to your school?'

She laughed. It was too absurd. 'Well, St Christopher's could certainly do with an injection of cash, but I haven't come here to ask for funding. I came here to tell you…to tell you…'

'I'm all ears, Alice. Take me somewhere new and challenging that explains your presence here.'

He sat forward, shot her a darkly wolfish smile, rested his arms on the desk and in a rush Alice said what she had come to say.

'I'm pregnant, Mateo. I came here to tell you that I'm having a baby.'

A deathly silence greeted this. It stretched and stretched and she could see his expression moving rapidly from shock to incredulity to outright disbelief.

'You can't be! Why would you come here and tell

me something like that? Absolute nonsense!' He stood up, his body as tense as a bowstring, dark brows furrowed in arrogant disbelief, every inch of him simmering with furious denial. 'I refuse to believe a word of what you're saying!'

Alice stared at him in silence. She'd wondered how he would react but complete denial hadn't been one of the options—although she'd been spot-on with the anger.

She took a deep breath to steady herself and offered him a tight, indifferent smile.

'Okay.'

'Okay? *Okay?*'

'I came here to tell you because it was the responsible thing to do.' She stood up and snatched her coat and backpack from where she had dumped them by the side of the chair. 'If you don't want to believe me, then no one's forcing you to. I didn't expect anything from you, anyway. Now, if you'll excuse me, I'm going to carry on with my day.'

'You'll do no such thing! You can't just waltz in here and drop a bombshell like that and then tell me you're leaving! Alice…*don't you dare!*'

Alice ignored him. She didn't look back. She began walking briskly out of his office, leaving him rising to his feet behind his desk. She could feel the sting of tears behind her eyes, because if she were certain of one thing it was this: never in a million years had she dreamt of having a baby by a guy who not only wanted nothing to do with her, but didn't even believe a word she said.

What was the opposite of 'happy ever after'? Whatever it was, she was definitely now living in that world.

No one knew about the pregnancy yet, but she was already projecting forward to telling her parents and seeing their disappointment. Of course they would try and hide it, and of course they would be supportive all the way, but she had let them down and the thought of it put a pain in her chest.

She fled.

Standing behind his desk, for the first time in his life Mateo was immobilised. Shock had drained him of the ability to think in a straight line.

Pregnant? No!

Those were the first thoughts that had run through his head when she had detonated that landmine. She couldn't be! He'd reacted with swift, instinctive denial as his mind had shut down.

And then she was half-running out of his office and here he was, still shell-shocked, but his brain was actually starting to engage. Why would she lie? She wasn't a liar. It just wasn't in her nature. And why would she have waited until now to find out who he was? If she'd been a mercenary gold-digger who'd somehow got a whiff of what he was made of, then why hadn't she contacted him sooner? And why wouldn't she have used the straightforward approach of trying to entice him back into bed?

She would have had to be crazy to make up a story about a pregnancy. She would have known that sooner or later she would be found out, and anyway, surely she must have suspected that he would insist on a pregnancy test, along with a medical examination and a DNA test?

And he knew, as well, that he had subconsciously

been catapulted back to that time when a surprise pregnancy had forced him down a road he hadn't foreseen, with all the predictable disastrous consequences. He'd been knocked for six but there was only the truth: she really *was* pregnant.

Mateo didn't stop to think about the repercussions of what she had told him. There would be plenty of time for that later. He exited his office at speed and handed his PA the very unusual task of finding out exactly where St Christophers was located. Then he waited, impatiently, for the full twenty minutes as she went into action, checking online and making calls, calling in at least two favours from friends who were teachers, making sure that when he showed up there would be no obstacles regarding entry.

Alice had run away from him but there was no way he wasn't going to find her. No way he was going to hang around and wait until she decided to get in touch with him again—*if* she decided to get in touch with him again. She'd come to do the decent thing and he'd reacted in just the sort of manner that would have had anyone in her position running for the hills. She'd come to deliver a message and he'd decided in his wisdom to shoot the messenger. He'd allowed shock, horror and a subconscious kneejerk reaction to something from his past dictate his response.

He remained in his office for half an hour more, thinking, allowing his head to be occupied with the practical issues surrounding the shock news. He avoided digging deeper into his own feelings about the thought of being a father. He didn't want to confront the feelings of vulnerability he had had all those years ago, the yearning and thrill of having a child only for those hopes to be dashed.

It was another hour and a half and just after lunch by the time he made it to the school and was instantly ushered in, having had the head pre-warned of his visit. His PA had pulled some strings, but Mateo thought he would have been able to get in without that simply because he was who he was. His identity could easily be checked and he could have promised a sizeable donation.

He looked around at the shabby surroundings masked by cheerful banners and upbeat sayings printed boldly on bright pieces of card and artwork stuck on the walls in neat rows on either side of a corridor teeming with kids coming and going. An inner-city school in desperate need of refurbishment, relying on government funding and donations from strangers. These were the sort of surroundings he hadn't been exposed to in a very, very long time and when he thought of Alice, actually imagining that she might have to face raising their child on a teacher's wage, his heart squeezed tight. He would definitely be doing something to improve the place.

But all that for later. For now, Alice.

Alice was so absorbed in thinking about Mateo and his shock and horror at what she had told him that she kept losing track of what the kids were doing. Just now, four in the back row were passing notes between them and giggling. The rest had their heads down and were doing their best to ignore the unruly back row.

Clara, her teaching assistant, was sitting with three

children around her, painstakingly going over some work which they were finding impossible to comprehend.

A normal day, but not for her. What happened next? She'd done what she'd known she had to do. She'd told Mateo about the baby, but it was clear from how he'd reacted that he wasn't going to take any kind of active part in its upbringing. He had his gilded life, a life in which long-term commitment was not allowed to intrude, and there was nothing more long-term than a child. So he'd gone into denial mode and she had to accept that he might just stay there.

When she thought about the nuts and bolts of having a baby when she earned a modest income and rented a place, she could feel a headache coming on. She would have to move back home and live with her parents until she found her feet.

With those thoughts buzzing in her head, she was only aware of someone at the door when the entire class fell silent. The four at the back, all girls, were staring at the door with their mouths open and, as Alice slowly turned around, she knew who was at the door. Only one person could inspire that sort of reaction, and it wasn't Mr Dennis the headmaster. He might inspire a bit of temporary silence but definitely no jaws on the ground.

Mateo.

He was lounging in the doorway, the very embodiment of sexiness, his brooding, green eyes lasered on her, and she could feel bright colour surge into her cheeks.

They could have heard a pin drop.

'We need to talk,' he drawled from the doorway.

Someone from the back row piped up in a 'butter wouldn't melt' voice, 'Miss, is that your boyfriend?'

Alice leapt to her feet, threw a stern look around her, told them that she would be back in ten minutes and then walked quickly towards Mateo, eager to usher him away from her gawping pupils. They might struggle to remember some basic rules of maths, but they would have memories like elephants when it came to remembering *this*.

Alice felt a wave of anger rush through her. First he had told her that he didn't believe a word she'd told him and now, here he was in *her* territory! If he thought that he could pursue a conversation about her making stuff up then he was in for a shock.

She didn't glance behind her as she restrained herself from slamming the classroom door. Nor did she utter a single word as she dragged him down the corridor, quieter now that there was no change of class in progress, but still not empty.

There were three quiet rooms used for one-to-one teaching. She took him to an empty one now and shut the door behind her but she remained leaning against it while he turned to look at her.

'First of all,' he said before she could lay into him, 'I want to apologise.'

CHAPTER SIX

'SIT.' SHE POINTED to one of the chairs ringed round a small square table, the surface of which was scuffed with the markings of pens over the years. He dwarfed the room and oozed the sort of expensive sophistication that emphasised the shabbiness of his surroundings: bare green walls in need of repainting, a couple of posters with inspirational quotes from well-known books and a weathered low-shelving system that was stuffed with various educational books and leaflets.

Alice looked at him and felt that familiar lurch in her stomach, a purely visceral awareness of him as a man, as someone who had made love to her, a guy who appealed on the most basic level—whatever her head had to say about it.

'You had no right to come here.'

'I had every right to come here. You detonated a bomb in my life. This isn't the place to have this sort of conversation. Have you had lunch? I can take you somewhere a little less…confined…and we can at least relax and discuss this situation in a bit of comfort.'

'I thought you'd already made yourself perfectly clear on where you stood with *this situation*.'

'I apologise. I…may have overreacted but it wasn't something I was expecting. Alice, let's get out of here. Someone is going to barge in at any minute, and neither of us is going to be able to give what has to be discussed the attention it deserves if we're listening out for someone pushing that door open.'

'I haven't finished for the day.'

'Then finish.'

'Don't think you can come here and tell me what to do!'

Mateo didn't answer. He stood up and began heading towards the door.

'Where are you going?'

'To the staff room. I have a good idea where it is. The teacher who showed me to your classroom helpfully gave me a little tour of the school. I may have mentioned that I was interested in making a financial contribution.'

'You can't go to the staff room!'

'I can when you consider that I'm going to explain the situation to your fellow colleagues. I'm sure they'll understand why we may want a little privacy to discuss this development.'

He looked at her and she returned his calm, level gaze with biting frustration.

'You're…*impossible*!'

'That's what I call a massive overstatement, all things considered,' Mateo returned coolly. 'So, what are you going to do?'

'Wait for me by the front doors.' Alice gritted her teeth. 'I'll join you in ten minutes.'

She rushed to the staff room, said something about

a personal situation arising out of the blue and made it to the front doors of the school before her time was up.

Mateo was staring through the glass doors and she stopped abruptly and took a few seconds to look at him. Her heart was beating like a sledgehammer. He'd hunted her down and she could feel some of the heavy weight of uncertainty lift from her shoulders.

Whatever the state of their affairs, it could only be a good thing for him to acknowledge his child. Good for him, but mostly good for this baby they had accidentally created. As a teacher, Alice had seen many times the effect on children of broken homes, absent parents and just mothers or fathers unwilling or unable to provide the security their offspring needed.

She had seen it all. It was one thing if a parent had died, or even if a couple had loved and tried but lost the battle and divorced. It was another thing completely if one parent had just decided to walk away from their own flesh and blood and not look back. That was the sort of thing that always came out eventually and could cause lasting damage.

He might have reacted forcefully and negatively to what she had sprung on him, but Mateo wasn't running away, and she felt as though some of her faith in him had been restored. She grudgingly conceded that, if he had gone into instant denial mode at what she had thrown at him, then it was only to be expected. He was a guy who controlled every aspect of his life. Of course he wasn't going to embrace the least controlled event ever to have happened to him with open arms and a warm, trusting smile.

She powered herself towards him as he turned to look at her.

'I've ordered a cab to take us somewhere a little more private.'

'I know this is a shock, Mateo, but I couldn't think of any other way to do it.'

'You realise I'll be taking nothing on trust. I'll want you to have a full medical examination so that I have all the facts at my disposal.'

'What sort of facts? Are you still going with the theory that I showed up at your office pretending to be having your baby?'

They walked to the black cab waiting by the kerb and she slid into the back seat, making space for him next to her. Every nerve in her body was stretched taut with anxiety and tension…and a dark, feverish excitement she couldn't shake.

'I'm not going with that theory,' Mateo said seriously. He angled his body against the car door so that he could look at her levelly.

'Ah, I see. You think that I've been sleeping with someone else and now I'm trying to palm their child off as yours so that I can… I don't know…force you into parting with your precious cash for a baby that isn't yours?'

'These things happen,' Mateo muttered, but as their eyes tangled he could see the senselessness of that misplaced caution. She wouldn't do that. He might be primed to distrust, but to distrust *her* would be downright offensive…

He was going to be a father!

There was no point harking back to those dark days when impending fatherhood had forced him down a path he wouldn't have taken, and when gut-wrenching disappointment at Bianca's miscarriage had cut so deeply. This was the here and now and positioning himself on the opposite side of the fence to her was not a good way to start.

He unconsciously glanced at her stomach, wondering what it would feel like to see it expanding with his child. He refused to succumb to the thrill of anticipation. He remembered what that had felt like, the vulnerability that had come with it and the anguish when things had collapsed. He had withdrawn behind his barriers then, but he'd always known that he'd taken it a damn sight harder than Bianca had.

'I don't understand how this happened,' he said in low, calm voice. 'Precautions were taken. I'm a very careful man.'

'Not *all the time*,' Alice reminded him uncomfortably. 'Once or twice things got a little out of hand… One morning, very early, we were both half-asleep… You reached out and…'

'I remember.' He flushed darkly. He'd never felt passion like he had for those few days when he'd been marooned with her in his lodge…and, yes, once or twice contraception had been an afterthought.

'Or maybe it was just a genuine accident…a tear in a condom. It happens.'

'Look, we'll be at my club in a few minutes. Let's park the details until we get there. How…how have you been?'

'Wonderful.'

'And your parents? Were they worried when you told them about your little adventure?'

'I thought it best not to mention anything although, now that I'm having a baby, I suppose I'll have to confess to what happened.'

'You haven't told them yet?'

'It was only right, as the father of this baby, that you were the first to know and I only found out about the pregnancy myself a couple of days ago.'

'It must have been a shock.' He could only admire her calmness. She had done what she thought was the right thing to do and hadn't showed up at his office with accusations, blame or demands for money. 'All right, look, there will be no tests to determine paternity. Of course I believe you. It was the shock talking. What we have to do now is decide what the way forward is going to be.' He glanced past her. 'We're here. We can talk about this once we're inside. This is as private as it gets.'

The cab had slowed in front of a door in a wall. Alice frowned, confused, because this wasn't what she'd been expecting.

'Your club?'

'Probably the most private place in London and numbers are strictly limited. This is where the world is run.'

'You're kidding.'

'Only slightly.'

She fell back as he pulled out an old-fashioned metal key and let them in, standing back so that she could precede him. Inside, the corridor was dark, cool and silent, a space of flagstone tiles and panelling that ran halfway up. The lighting was subdued and, when she began to wonder where the heck they were, they turned left into an open space guarded by a weathered guy behind a desk who nodded at Mateo without moving.

'Sir.'

'Fornby. Doing well?'

'As well as can be expected, given the times we live in.'

'All a man can ask for.'

They'd left the madness of London behind and somehow entered a different place in a different era. This, Alice thought, trying hard not to gape, was what extreme wealth bought: perfect privacy. Somewhere where a person could be a direct descendent of Zeus and no one would glance in their direction.

It was tough not looking around at the clusters of deep sofas and tables discreetly set apart. Some were occupied. A glance at one of the occupants relaxing with a newspaper revealed a personality who had been in the news for the past fortnight, a man in charge of fractious talks with certain nations in the Middle East. Two showbiz personalities were talking and eating food, and there was a small group of two women and a man, all besuited, poring over a bank of documents with a bottle of wine on the table between them.

No one looked at Alice and Mateo as they settled into two deep chairs with a circular table in front of them. A man appeared from nowhere with a bottle of sparkling mineral water. Mateo ordered a carafe of 'red wine': obviously the kind of red he liked had long been noted, presumably with no deviation unless told otherwise.

She murmured something about the water being fine. 'Wow,' she whispered. 'I never knew places like this existed.'

'Most people don't. London is full of exclusive clubs but this one thrives on being very much under the radar.'

'It's definitely more private than the room at the school.' It was quiet and dark, with rich, old furnishings and the sort of carpets that looked as though they belonged in the age of the Tudors. The men serving food and drinks had a palpable air of expertise and discretion.

They sat back as a tray of canapés was brought for them. Frankly, Alice would have liked to carry on surreptitiously staring around her, but reluctantly she returned to Mateo, who was now looking at her with a certain amount of amusement.

But it didn't last long. 'I think we should both be as professional as possible in the way we approach this situation,' he opined.

Alice focused. Of course, this was exactly the right way to deal with the situation. They'd had a fling but, beyond that, it wasn't as though he had feelings for her. It wouldn't do to forget that, when she had suggested carrying on with what they had to see where it would lead, he had firmly closed the conversation down and sent her on her way.

If they handled this in a *professional* way, then they could remain friends, which was what would be necessary as time went on. They would have a bond that would never go away, whatever their changes in fortune.

And yet her heart constricted at all the consequences that lay down that road. She'd have to watch as other women came and went in his life, knowing when that *someone* he had talked about came along—that woman with whom he would want to share his life, who wouldn't be under any illusions that he was going to fall in love with her—Alice would wave goodbye to their daughter or son and watch him drive away with someone else in the passenger seat.

'Neither of us expected this to happen,' Mateo started, 'but I intend to pull my weight every inch of the way. First of all, there will never be any need for you to worry about money. My child will want for nothing. I knew what *want* was when *I* was a child, and it's a miserable hardship that I'm only grateful my own flesh and blood will not have to endure. And, as his mother, you will likewise want for nothing. You will both have the best.'

'I'm not asking for anything for myself, Mateo,' Alice said faintly.

'You don't have to. It goes without saying that you can give up your teaching job, which I imagine doesn't pay the earth.'

'That won't be happening.'

'Your thoughts on that might change. You might find that you enjoy being a hands-on mother when you no longer need to go out and earn a pittance teaching. On the subject of which, you were right—your school could do with an injection of funds from the looks of it. Before we part company, I'll get details the name of your admin person so that I can do my civic duty.'

Alice was beginning to feel as if she had suddenly jumped on a rollercoaster and was now whizzing madly across the universe.

'Well, I'm sure the principal would be grateful for any financial help… Fund-raising can only get so far, so thank you; and, yes, it would be nice knowing that our child will be financially secure.'

It was all so matter-of-fact. They could have been discussing a business deal, she thought sadly. The intense physical chemistry between them had been wiped out and replaced with this run-of-the-mill conversation about their future.

'I don't suppose this was what you'd spent your life looking forward to,' Mateo said roughly.

'I'd always planned on having children.'

'But not like this—an unplanned pregnancy with a man you never banked on having a future with.'

'And who never banked on having a future with me.'

'Or with anyone,' Mateo qualified. 'But, love and marriage aside, I want you to know that you can expect one hundred percent support from me.'

Alice picked at the wonderful canapés and wondered why they tasted of cardboard. Why did she feel so miserable? He was being terrific. She couldn't have asked for more. Was it because, for her, having a baby had always been wrapped up with love and marriage? Just something she'd always taken for granted?

Or did this businesslike approach hurt because here she was, carrying his baby, and she wanted so much more than financial support. Once upon a time, she had dimly seen Simon in this position. Now she knew that what she felt for Simon had not been love. She'd had a narrow escape but, from the frying pan she'd fallen straight into the fire, because, yes, what she felt for this wonderful, elusive, complex guy sitting within touching distance was love in all its glory—but love that wasn't reciprocated. He was offering her emotional support, and she knew that he would be there for her, but only *because of the baby.*

'I appreciate that,' Alice said politely.

'Can I...see it?'

'See what?'

'The baby. Now.' He flushed darkly. 'A scan.'

'Don't tell me you still have doubts about that?'

'I don't. I just want to...'

'Okay,' Alice agreed in a husky voice. 'I'll get it arranged.'

'And then we can fine-tune all the details. I don't know where you live, Alice, but I'm guessing it's not a palace. And before you tell me that you don't need a palace to raise a child, you're going to move from wherever you are to something suitable, and that is non-negotiable. Also non-negotiable is that you use the money I intend to deposit into your account. The only thing that's negotiable there is the sum, if it's not enough. Like I said, I intend to take care of both of you in style.'

'I'm very grateful, Mateo.'

'Then why are you looking at me as though I'm the Grinch who stole Christmas?'

'Because it all sounds so much like a business deal...'

Mateo glanced down, lush lashes concealing his expression, making him a closed book.

It did, he privately conceded, but wasn't this the best route forward—the one that avoided a future that would probably be filled with messy complications? Hadn't he raced into a youthful marriage because of a pregnancy without foreseeing all the chaos that would result from his hasty decision? Had he and Bianca had that baby, wouldn't the whole thing have come unstuck in an ugly and predictable way? Yes. And the ugly unravelling of a marriage would always impact a child far more than two parents who liked and respected one another and worked in unison for the good of the child they had created without aiming for what was never going to be achieved.

Mateo knew that he had locked away his heart, just as he knew that it would be unfair to encourage Alice to do the same with hers, which was what would happen if they made the mistake of marrying. For him, marriage would be something that might or might not happen one day and, when that day arrived, it would be a choice made with his head.

Alice deserved better. She deserved to have the best she could find and that would be to marry someone for love and not through necessity.

He thought of her with another man and bit down a rush of jealousy. It was an emotion so foreign to him that he almost didn't recognise it for what it was.

'What are you thinking?'

Mateo looked at her thoughtfully. 'Isn't that how it should be, Alice? I know we had…a good time for a while but that wasn't about love. That was about sex. What you want for yourself isn't to be with a guy you don't love who is as cynical as you are optimistic…' He smiled crookedly at her.

Again he felt that sharp pang of something strike deep into his core when he thought of her with another man. It went against all the cool logic that had been the bedrock of his adult life and he refused to let it in for closer inspection. It unsettled him. In his head, vulnerability like that led to love, and love led to loss. He would never invite the possibility of loss back into his life.

'Of course you're right, and I'm really glad you're being so…accommodating about this. I know it's the last thing you need.'

'I can arrange for you to have a private scan,' Mateo inserted in a rough, uncertain voice. 'Please.'

Alice's smile was slow and genuine. She would have to face certain facts, however hard it was going to be. He didn't think she had feelings for him but she did: deep, strong feelings that had wrapped around every bit of her heart. However, he had none for her, aside from feelings of responsibility now. He would take care of her because she was carrying his child, and of course he was right: for her, marriage without love would be awful. So the conventional situation she had always envisaged for herself was not to be…

But he *had* come to terms with impending fatherhood much quicker than she could ever have hoped. Not only that, for him to be so keen on a scan showed that he was facing up to this sudden bomb dropped into his well-ordered life full-on, without trying to distance himself from it. And that was to be celebrated.

A lot of men would have turned their backs in a scenario such as this.

'Yes, sure.'

'And then we can really sit down and talk about what exactly happens next…'

The scan was arranged for the following week— a private scan, in a private hospital. As Alice was ushered through to where Mateo was waiting for her, she was afforded a glimpse of life that happened on the other side of the wealth divide. The hospital was quiet and luxurious. There were no trolleys spilling out of corridors and no sense of frantic urgency with patients, nurses, doctors and consultants racing through corridors, white coats flying and noise and bustle everywhere.

Mateo turned around. She paused as their eyes met and he rose to walk towards her. He'd phoned her every day since their last meeting. He'd asked her about her day, how she was, what she'd eaten. Alice knew that his concern was for the baby but she was treacherously becoming accustomed to seeing his name pop up on her phone and hearing the dark, velvety sound of his low, sexy and hypnotising voice.

He'd come from work and was in a suit, a cashmere tan coat draped over the chair next to him. Her heart skipped several beats as he neared her, and just for a few seconds it was easy to pretend that this was a normal relationship, a loving relationship with the man who was to be father of her child.

He gave her a peck on the cheek. If there was any reminder needed that their relationship had changed, then this was it. A peck on the cheek was a far cry from the hot lust that had made it impossible for him to keep his hands off her.

'This is like a five-star hotel,' Alice whispered, eyeing the neatly turned out consultants occasionally walking past and the cool, unruffled receptionists waiting to usher them to the right place.

'No need to whisper.' Mateo drew back and looked down at her. 'And it's a taste of what you'll be getting used to.'

'I'm fine with the health care the state provides.'

'Again, this is one of those non-negotiables. Have you cleared your diary for the day? I'd like to take you for an early dinner so that we can discuss some of the finer details of what comes next for us. Not my club— we can skip that—somewhere more casual.'

'Yes, I've taken the afternoon off.' Alice was trying to digest the way things had changed between them. They were as polite as strangers. The peck on the cheek had had the sting of indifference. He was no longer attracted to her and the teasing familiarity between them that had built so quickly and effortlessly when they'd been snowbound was a thing of the past.

And this was what she would have to get used to. He generously wanted the best for her, and had approached what had been thrown at him in an adult and thoughtful way. She should be grateful, not quietly devastated.

'Good.'

It was said in a clipped voice, with polite, unreadable gaze and kind smile. She wondered whether he had moved on from her and was seeing someone else. A bit of background reading on him had told a story of a guy who had a healthy appetite when it came to the opposite sex.

They were escorted to the maternity ward and to the bank of quiet, comfortable rooms where scans were done. Her mind was still on Mateo and the business of getting used to this version of him as she lay on the couch, suddenly self-conscious as the procedure began. He'd seen her naked. They had made love many times and he had touched her in all her most intimate places. Even so, lying on this couch in a darkened room, with the machine beeping and the radiographer about to see what was happening inside her, Alice felt oddly nervous and vulnerable.

But all of that was forgotten when she saw the little speck on the machine, the fierce pumping of a tiny heart, the beginnings of a boy or girl. The radiographer was talking, and Alice excitedly asked a couple of questions, but it was only when they were wrapping up the scan that she realised that Mateo had not said a word. He'd been completely silent and, as they were left on their own to digest what they'd been told and gaze at the black and white picture printed out for them, she suddenly felt her heart drop.

She couldn't meet his eyes as she hurriedly hopped off the couch and straightened her clothes. 'It's all very real now, isn't it?' she said in a high, light voice. She backed away so that she was pressed against the couch, arms folded, her eyes locked with his.

'Come again?'

'It's okay to discuss the ramifications of a baby but, now that you've actually seen proof of the pregnancy with your own eyes, I guess all those ways your life is going to change are really being rammed home to you.'

He was pale. Good intentions were easily washed away, she thought miserably. He'd been great talking about what an active parent he was going to be, but was he now considering the consequences in a slightly different way? A living, breathing little human would take up a disproportionate amount of time and it was a responsibility that would never end.

Was he now back-tracking on being hands-on and heading down the 'financial support only' route?

Surely not? And yet, why on earth was he not saying anything?

'If you've changed your mind about…about everything, then that's fine. I understand,' she said in a rush, grabbing her coat and back pack and walking briskly to the door whilst making sure to keep plenty of room between them. Get too close, and whatever vibe he had just went right through her, scrambling her brain and turning her body to mush. Right now, she wasn't interested in either of those things happening.

'Well?' The silence from him was agonising. 'Have you—changed your mind? Because you can come right out and say it.'

'Let's get out of here. When it comes to conversations, a hospital is only marginally better than a box room at a school.'

'I'm not going anywhere until you tell me what's going on, Mateo. If you're having second thoughts about getting involved with this baby, then that's fine, but I'm not going to go for dinner so that we can discuss your change of mind over a three-course meal.'

He was already heading out and Alice tripped along next to him, every nerve in her body braced for news that was going to be so disappointing. If thinking about a future with him involved in her life at some level had been bad, thinking about a future with him *not* in her life, just depositing money into an account to make sure she was okay, was a million times worse.

'You're right.' Mateo finally spoke when they were outside and a black cab was slowing for them. 'Slight change of plan. In the cab, Alice. This isn't an email conversation, I'm afraid, or anything I want to rush because you're suddenly in a hurry. Restaurant chit chat with a waiter interrupting us every three minutes isn't going to do—not quite the venue for the conversation we need to have.'

He stepped aside, waiting until she had no option but to slide into the taxi. While she grappled with the near impossibility of remaining silent, he stared, first at her, with cool, assessing eyes, then straight ahead.

Alice fumed and simmered in silence as they cleared through late afternoon traffic, stopping and starting before cruising past the crowded streets into a hushed residential setting where towering Georgian houses were set back from the road by a wide pavement. Rows of precise, black wrought-iron railings stood guard outside each of the impressive properties.

'Where the heck are we, Mateo?'

'My house.'

'No way.'

'I'm not having an argument in the back of a cab, Alice, so hop out. You're free to argue with me when we get inside.'

'That won't be happening because I won't be getting inside.'

But, agonisingly, she knew that she would because she needed to hear what Mateo had to say. Running from a problem never helped when it came to solving it. A baby was on the way and neither hurt feelings nor stubborn pride should be allowed to get in the way of deciding what to do.

His house was testimony to his immense wealth. In comparison, his lodge on those snowy slopes had been a positive shack in comparison. Alice winced when she thought of her kindly remarks to him when she'd thought that he was no more than an averagely well paid IT guy who might only be able to afford a nifty ski lodge if it was rented out when he wasn't there and who probably didn't own his own place in London.

She stepped into a glorious sea of white marble, bold abstract paintings on the walls and rich, expensive rugs underfoot. A very modern staircase of metal and glass carved its way upstairs, dissecting the open area into two halves. Wide-eyed, she gazed around her. To the left, an impressive archway led to various rooms. On the right, an arch that mirrored it led to yet more rooms. Why on earth did one guy need so many rooms? she wondered.

Her gaze finally settled on him and he raised his eyebrows and told her that they could chat in the sitting room.

'You have a lovely…er…house, Mateo. Or maybe I should say *palace*.'

She blinked when he burst out laughing, and then blushed, because the sound of that laughter, rich and amused, was at once familiar and filled her with nostalgia.

It was also a timely reminder of the silence that had settled over him ever since the scan. Which in turn brought her right back down to earth with a bump.

'So…' she ventured as she was ushered into an amazing sitting room with low, cream sofas and a warm, rich rug that covered most of the floor.

'So…'

Mateo raked his fingers through his hair and looked at her gravely as she edged towards one of the chairs and sank into it. He sat facing her and leant forward, arms resting loosely on his thighs.

That scan had changed everything. He and Bianca had married in haste when she had only just become pregnant and there had been no scan. The usual confirmation tests, yes, but no scan at that stage…and then the miscarriage had changed everything. Plus he'd been so young, already tough, but not nearly as tough as he was now. He'd thought about fatherhood, and had known that he would always do the right thing, but the whole concept of a baby and the reality of it had been abstract and woolly—something that would happen down the line.

But seeing that little scrap of life eagerly waiting to enter the world… Mateo had felt the fierce tug of possessiveness that had wiped out all good intentions about stepping back because he didn't want to pull her into the loveless marriage she wouldn't want. No. He had seen his baby and in an instant had known that anything less than marriage wasn't going to do.

It had been naïve to think otherwise but then he was so accustomed to boxing up his emotions that he hadn't expected to feel the overpowering jolt he had felt in that room. Nothing could have protected him from it, not even the hard veneer he had cultivated over the years. More than anything else, he'd seen that tiny beating heart and had known that keeping Alice safe, keeping their baby safe, would be his lifelong mission, and to do that he would not be able to step back. Detachment was no longer an option.

How could he ever have thought that he could allow another man to enter her life and join in decision making about *his* child's future? How could he ever have imagined that anyone but him could be involved with this baby of theirs?

He looked at her carefully and knew that, having approached the situation with the emotionalism of a robot, he was going to have to win her over. He'd magnanimously told her that he would be a hands-on father but in the capacity of one who lived a separate life—that she needed to fulfil her dream of finding someone to love and he would give her the freedom to do that.

He was going to do a complete turnaround and already he wondered why he hadn't gone down this route in the first place. He'd remembered Bianca, remembered the foolhardiness of rushing into marriage for the sake of a pregnancy and then all the attendant problems that had resulted from his hasty, emotional decision. He'd then obeyed his instinct and turned away from making a similar mistake.

But Alice wasn't Bianca. They might no longer be together, but the relationship hadn't been poisonous. He and Alice could make a go of it, but he would have to persuade her. Somehow he would have to make her see that there was life beyond love. No way was he going to walk away from the one hundred percent commitment that now beckoned.

'Well? Are you going to say anything, Mateo? Like I said, I didn't come to your office because I wanted anything from you. If you've had a reality check now that we've had that scan, then just come out and tell me.'

'I've had a reality check, Alice.'

'And…'

'And this is going to play out slightly differently. We're going to get married.'

CHAPTER SEVEN

ALICE LOOKED AT HIM in shock. The shock was then followed by confusion. Was this the same guy who had, only days before, banged on about the situation requiring a businesslike approach? Since when had marriage been *businesslike*? Weren't *business deals* more along the lines of shaking hands and signing a contract?

'I can see you're surprised.'

'Not what I was expecting, no.'

'Seeing our baby, Alice, brought it forcibly home to me that this isn't something that can be dealt with the way I would deal with a work problem.'

'Well, Mateo, you don't say.' But her heart was beating like a sledgehammer. *Marriage!* It was everything she had dreamed of. The guy she loved…their baby…

She had sneaked a glance at Mateo in that small, darkened room and her heart had swelled with love as she drank in the beautiful lines of his face cast into shadows. Then she had looked at the small, living, breathing baby they had created together and the longing for them to be a family unit, a *real* family unit, had been so overwhelming that she'd had to breathe in deeply to control the rush of emotion.

And now, the prospect of marrying this guy was being dangled in front of her like a carrot. She thought of them bringing home their baby, buying stuff for their home together, stuff that wouldn't be white or include any marble. She thought of them watching telly, going to the shops together, having friends and family to dinner…

When she blinked, what she saw was über-luxury all around her and a man who lived firmly in this world. A world that was a million miles from the dream world she had just concocted in her head. So much about this picture was right but so much more was wrong.

If the promise of normality with Simon had not been enough for her in the end…if she had, in fact, wanted something more extraordinary…then at the very heart of her, she knew that it would only be okay with a guy who truly loved her. What she'd found was extraordinary without the love. She longed for this extraordinary man but with the wonderful *ordinariness* of love. In the end, love was what made the small trivia in life oh, so amazing.

Mateo had been moved by seeing his own flesh and blood on that scan, just as she had. Now he was prepared to go a step further and offer her the one thing she knew he would never, ever have offered in any other circumstances: a ring. However much she longed to take that ring and slip it on her finger, how could she do it? How could she turn his world on its head and live with herself? He didn't love her. Would she be able to cope with that for ever?

How long before they started wandering around this

big, palatial house like two strangers bound together for the sake of the child they shared? How long before the isolation of doing the small things on her own began to eat away at all their noble intentions about being united for the sake of their baby? Would either of them be happy?

'That's not going to work, Mateo,' she said gently. 'Although I appreciate the offer.'

'I realise this was never your Plan A, Alice, but it makes sense and I should have seen that from the very beginning. Let me get you something to drink: tea? Fresh juice? Water?'

'Let's just talk this out, Mateo. No, you're right, I never thought that I'd be having a baby out of wedlock, for want of a better way of putting it. You know, it just wasn't something that was ever on the radar.' She sighed wryly. 'That along with spending a few torrid nights with a complete stranger.'

'But now we're here and I feel that we need to both put our Plan As to one side and consider what's best for the baby. And that's both parents on board, married and united in making joint decisions and providing stability and security.'

'Love is what makes a marriage work, or else it's just as good for us to live apart and amicably share in this baby's upbringing. We can like one another and get along without tying ourselves together. We both know the tie would break eventually, anyway.' She sighed and looked around her, this time more slowly, before resting her eyes on him.

'That's not what you said when we were at my lodge,'

Mateo countered with silky assurance. 'If I recall, you said that you wanted to see where our relationship led when we returned to London.'

'Yes, well, that was then. That was before…'

'Yes, things are different now, but what we had… Let's be honest, it's still there, isn't it? It is for me. When you showed up at my office, when I saw you again, I wondered whether that thing I'd felt might have disappeared… that *charge*.'

'Mateo, this is beside the point…'

She watched with alarm and excitement as he rose slowly from where he'd been sitting and sauntered towards her, dragging a foot stool which he placed so close to her that she could feel the heat emanating from him. 'Is it?'

His eyes were dark, questioning and gently probing and they stirred a longing in her that was dangerously familiar.

'What does it matter if this so-called charge is there or not?' Alice whispered a little shakily. 'Would you have done something about it if I'd shown up to ask you to pick things back up with us?'

'I would have tried not to.'

His blunt honesty hurt but it showed a side of him that was to be commended. He didn't play games. What he said would always be the truth.

'Because you're so attracted to me, right?'

'Yes, as a matter of fact.' His eyes were lazy, roving over her flushed face in a leisurely, sexy scrutiny. 'I would have been tempted but I would have probably reacted with my head and not that other unreliable part of my body. I would have known that I couldn't offer you the long-term relationship you wanted. Even when you told me about the pregnancy, when I knew that I had to allow you the freedom to find a man who could give you what you really wanted in life, even then, I wanted you. But I resisted the urge to touch, to try and seduce you…to tempt you back into my arms.'

He edged closer fractionally, leaning slightly into her. 'But things are different now. Now I want to offer you a long-term relationship.'

'I never said I wanted a long-term relationship with you. I said we could carry on having fun when we got back to London. I always knew you weren't the kind of long-term guy I was looking for.' Alice looked away and licked her lips. Her eyes strayed to the knees almost touching hers and the strong, brown hand hanging over one knee.

Mateo pressed his thumbs to his eyes and then looked at her, deadly serious. 'Having fun? No. I knew that would have been a bad idea. I'm not the sort of guy you would want to have fun with. You'd end up getting hurt.'

'Who's to say *I* would have been the one getting hurt?'

'I'm well-insulated when it comes to women having that sort of effect on me. But who knows…?' His green eyes darkened with wicked amusement. 'Think you might have been the one to make me cry, Alice?'

'I guess we'll never know!' She went bright red.

'At any rate, things have changed. This isn't about fun. This is about the baby we've made. I thought I could live with a situation whereby we shared this baby as friends, nothing more, but I can't. Seeing our baby moving inside you, that small speck...' He shook his head. 'We could work, Alice. I respect you, I like you, we get along and then...' he brushed her cheek with his finger '...there's this.'

'Mateo...' Alice heard the husky tremor in her voice and half-closed her eyes, tilting back her head, utterly unable to resist the pull of an attraction that was too powerful for her. His finger on her cheek was soft and gentle and the breath caught in her throat when that finger found the contour of her lips and delicately traced them.

'Kiss me,' she heard herself groan and he did. He kissed her. She'd forgotten just how sweet and beautiful the feel of his mouth was on hers. Cool lips and the slide of his tongue roused her until she was squirming and wet for him. When he rested his hand on her thigh, she immediately parted her legs, wanting more. Instead, frustratingly, he pulled back and looked at her gravely.

'We have more going for us than a hell of a lot of starry-eyed couples who start off with nothing more than the hope that a bit of fairy dust is going to last a lifetime.'

'A little fairy dust never hurt anyone...'

'Until it turns to shards of glass.'

'You're so cynical, Mateo.'

'Realist. And realism is what is going to work so well for us. Marry me, Alice. You'll find that I can make an excellent father and husband.'

Alice looked at him. There was so much going for what he had said—a stable life for a child who had not asked to be conceived. He would be a good provider and she knew that he would be an attentive husband. Her parents would be overjoyed; they were traditionalists through and through. And, yes, there was the sex. It would fade away, of course, and without love would slide into a sort of brother-sister amicability.

Inevitably, he would discreetly fool around. That went without saying. Duty would bind him to her but mutual respect, liking one another and having a child together would only go so far when it came to tethering him. He would be able to deal with the intensity of desire and the searing urge to protect what he would see as his, but would he be able to deal with the everyday normality that every relationship needed? Or would that bore him? Could an extraordinary man ever know the value of ordinary? And, however much she knew that she wanted and needed some extraordinariness in her life—that *something* that was all wrapped up with *love*—didn't she also know that normality was also needed to be in the mix?

Her heart would be crushed on a daily basis and, whilst Alice knew that she should put their child first, the thought of her own projected misery filled her with panic and apprehension. Maybe if she stood back she might be able to build her own inner reinforcements to protect her from that. Would she get stronger and more immune to his pull over time? Wasn't time supposed to do stuff like that?

'I'm not willing to make such a big commitment just yet, Mateo.'

'I'm not following you. Is it the love angle? Alice,

there's more to a successful marriage than love. We have all the ingredients to make it work, and that's not even taking into account the fact that we're still hot for one another.'

'It's not that. Maybe when you first decided that we were better off apart, free to see where life took us while remaining committed to our child, I thought about it and realised that it made sense.'

Their eyes tangled and she saw that in that instant Mateo knew that he had lost the argument. If he wanted marriage, he was going to have to win her over. And the only thing she wanted was the one thing he couldn't give her.

Alice was flicking through the paper in the staffroom three weeks later when she froze.

Three of her friends were busy marking papers and she was waiting for Mateo to show up because he wanted to show her something. He wouldn't say what.

She'd done her best to curb her excitement because she hadn't failed to notice that, ever since his heady marriage proposal, all had gone quiet on that particular front. She'd backed off and he'd immediately respected the distance she had insisted on keeping between them.

No more talk of the burning desire that simmered between them and no gentle persuasion for her to come round to his marriage solution. Had he actually been serious when he'd told her that he still fancied her, wanted her? Or had he decided that that was the best route to take because he had changed his mind and wanted to put a ring on her finger?

The uncertainty tormented Alice but she knew that the best thing she could do for their relationship was to ignore it. If he had changed his mind, then there was nothing she could do about it and, in every other aspect, he was turning out to be the responsible guy he had held himself out to be.

Besides, if the pull of that intense, crazy desire was snuffed out, then wouldn't that be all to the good? Wasn't that one complication removed?

He called her daily, saw her at least a couple of times a week and had insisted on relocating her from her rented place to somewhere more suitable. Alice had not objected, and the new place was so much more magnificent that she was quietly grateful that he had taken charge and stampeded through her weak protests that she was perfectly happy where she was. He'd also deposited a startling sum of money into her account, which he had labelled 'petty cash', and had opened several accounts for her at some of the high-end department stores.

He was as respectful and charming as any woman could have hoped for from the father of her unborn child and Alice struggled not to absolutely *hate it*. It was an adult, civilised relationship and she treacherously longed for the passion which had disappeared. No amount of bracing mantras could ease the anguish of having the man she adored so close and yet so far.

It hardly helped that when they had gone to see her parents, to jointly break the news to them, he had somehow managed to charm them into accepting what was presented as not marriage, but something sensible, loving and transparent—just as good in many ways.

The perfect guy. Except now, staring down at the pictures in the weekly gossip rag in front of her, the reality of their relationship was hitting home—because there he was, at some networking bash or other which he had attended the week before. And next to him, gazing up at him, was just the sort of leggy blonde he used to date before she'd come along.

She didn't want to keep staring at the pictures, looking for clues, so she slapped the magazine shut. But the images were imprinted in her head and they were still there, churning around, when Mateo buzzed her fifteen minutes later to tell her that he was waiting outside.

Mateo was lounging against his car, waiting for Alice to emerge. Winter had morphed into spring and there was a pleasant hint of warmth in the air. It was a source of wonder as to why she insisted on remaining in her job when there was no need.

'I like the people I work with,' she had told him doggedly, when he had probed her on that point. 'And I enjoy the kids, even though they can sometimes be unruly and stubborn. I love what I do and you can't expect me to give it all up just because I don't need the money any longer.'

Mateo was discovering what it was like to be with a woman who wasn't impressed with what he could provide. He'd steered clear of returning to the subject of marriage. He figured that, the more he made of it, the deeper she would dig in her heels, and maybe she would see sense if he resorted to the art of subtle persuasion, but he was beginning to wonder whether it was a ploy that was going to work.

Accustomed to getting his own way in everything, it went against the grain to play the long game but he could see no other way. He was dealing with a woman who was completely different from any woman he had ever known and in this instance he was on uncertain territory.

He'd had to back off, and back off he had. He'd ditched all talk of marriage and had been scrupulous when it came to not touching her or giving her any reason to think that he wanted to revive the physical side of their relationship. It felt as if he was starting from scratch, playing an urgent courting game, the rules of which he was not wholly sure about.

She had principles. Having met her parents, he could see where that had come from. He could see that what she wanted was to emulate the quiet love her parents shared. The more he thought about that, the more hopeless he felt about his quest to convince her that there were alternatives, and that those alternatives were workable and satisfactory—that within the framework of marriage lay a host of different ingredients; that there were no hard and fast rules that applied to everyone.

He saw her push through the glass door of the school and he straightened. She wore loose dark-grey trousers, a dark-grey jumper and serviceable flat shoes. It was the outfit of a working woman who put comfort above appearance and who had certainly done nothing in the way of dressing to impress because he was picking her up.

He walked towards her and had to resist the temptation to tuck some of those loose strands of hair behind her ears. The physical chemistry he felt buzzed like a live wire just beneath the surface of his polite conversation. Again, he was questioning his vow not to touch her. Was torturing himself like this even the right way to get what he wanted?

'How was your day?' he asked, relieving her of a backpack that seemed far too heavy for someone in her condition.

'Good, thank you. And yours?'

Mateo flicked her a curious, sideways glance as he picked up something in her tone of voice that was a little off-key.

'The usual,' he drawled. 'Stuck behind a desk making a shedload of money.'

'Anything else you've been doing recently?'

'Throw me some clues so that I can see where that question is going, would you?'

'It's not important. Where are you taking me? I hope it's nowhere fancy because I won't be changing into any party outfits. I'm tired after a hectic day at school, and honestly, all I really want to do is go home, have a shower, mark some homework and then go to bed.'

'Why on earth are you hanging onto that job? You're pregnant. You shouldn't be working your fingers to the bone.'

'We've already been through this, Mateo. I'm a normal person who enjoys doing a normal job. I'm not one of these glamorous types who thinks it's okay to swan around doing nothing but going to beauty parlours and attending fancy social dos.'

'Where the hell has *that* come from?'

'Nowhere,' Alice muttered. 'I'm just tired. Tell me where we're going.'

'It's a surprise but I'm hoping it'll be a pleasant one.'

He held open the door of his black BMW and she slid into the passenger seat.

Before he started the engine, he turned to her. 'Okay, spit it out. What's bothering you?'

'Nothing's bothering me.'

'Think I don't know you well enough to know when something's on your mind?'

'Honestly, Mateo, I'm just tired.'

She was the first to look away, and suddenly Mateo felt the vice-like grip of panic wrap around him. Was this a sign of her pulling away from him? Who knew what those friends and colleagues of hers talked about? Was she slowly being persuaded into taking the hard line that there was no way she would ever consider marriage?

He thought he'd left that door open for her to consider, to come to her senses. But had he? Should he have kept hammering home to her that marriage was the best solution, best for the baby? Should he have played hardball and seduced her into bed with him, put her in a place where walking away would have been a lot more difficult? Should he have ruthlessly exploited the fact that the chemistry wasn't just confined to him?

Maybe there was someone there, some teacher she was interested in, one of those touchy-feely, sensitive types providing a shoulder for her to cry on.

Unused to such flights of imagination, Mateo didn't quite know what to do with his thoughts. It took an effort for him to grapple his way back to a position of common sense. He shrugged and started the engine into life, and his powerful car purred away, cutting through the London traffic, heading south away from central London. When he glanced sideways at her, she was staring through the window. He wanted nothing more than to reach inside her head and find out what was going on in there.

They drove in silence, and it was only as they cleared the congested roads of London that she perked up and looked a little more curious about where they were going.

'I want to show you a house,' Mateo said, breaking the silence.

'A house?'

'You can't live in a rented place for ever. I've personally had a look around this place, and I think it's a good find. Although naturally, if you don't like it, then that's that.'

'We don't have the same taste in houses.'

Mateo heard the underlying cool in her voice and gritted his teeth.

'You like lots of white and marble, stuff with sharp edges—not very toddler-friendly.'

'My bachelor pad,' Mateo returned drily, 'wasn't meant to be toddler-friendly. I've always found I can manoeuvre round table corners without bumping into them and I rarely spill ice lollies on the white marble.'

'Not funny, Mateo. You might say your lifestyle isn't toddler-friendly.'

'Are you determined to pick an argument with me,

Alice? And, if you are, then maybe you could explain why so that I can defend myself?'

He pulled away from the main drag and began manoeuvring through the picturesque lanes and streets that circled the sprawl of Richmond Park.

Looking at him, Alice could feel the tension stiffening his shoulders and she knew that she was being unfair. So what if he was out there having a good time? So what if he was doing what he normally did, networking with beautiful blondes? She'd built up an entire scenario around a few photos in a stupid rag and had then needled away at him in a manner that was shamefully passive-aggressive—not like her at all.

He didn't deserve that. He'd been open and honest with her from the beginning and she could hardly find fault with whatever activities he decided to get up to in his own time. If anything, seeing those photos should have reminded her of his unsuitability long term. The player could never be taken away from the game for too long, and Mateo was a player at heart. Had he reconciled himself to that? The fact that they were in a 'no touching' place pretty much said it all.

Determined to be less emotional, she paid attention to where they were and, when he finally pulled up in front of a red-brick Victorian house in its little plot, she was open-mouthed with surprise.

'Not a single slab of marble in sight,' Mateo murmured, circling round the car to open her door for her. 'No sharp edges. Extremely toddler-friendly.'

'I'm sorry,' Alice said, looking at him and resting her hand on his arm. 'I haven't exactly been great company this afternoon.'

'To be discussed. Come in, have a look around and tell me what you think.'

Alice forgot about Mateo padding along slightly behind her as she explored the house. It was cosy, with little nooks and crannies leading to rooms in a topsy-turvy, charming way. There were wood floors throughout, and in the downstairs sitting room parquet flooring reminded her of where she had grown up in the vicarage. Outside, the garden was as tangled and charming as the inside had been, a broad stretch of lawn with fruit trees at the back growing against an old brick wall.

'It's perfect...' Alice breathed, finally turning to Mateo and smiling sheepishly. 'And not at all what I was expecting.'

They were walking back to his car and she glanced over her shoulder, already knowing that this was where she wanted to be. The sun was starting to lower in the sky, and her heart warmed when she looked sideways at Mateo, impressed at how he had managed to get something as big as this just right.

'I'm a guy who's full of surprises. I've booked a table for an early dinner for us so that we can discuss the place.'

'You assumed I'd like it?'

'I'd assumed even if you didn't that we would have a lot to discuss.'

As he circled the small courtyard in front of the

house heading out towards the town centre, Alice murmured, 'I haven't said how great it is that you've taken all this in your stride.'

Mateo looked at her in silence for a few seconds.

He'd made sure to take a step back as she'd looked around, wanting to gauge her reaction without her being aware of him gauging her reaction. She loved it, as he'd known she would; subtle persuasion had been his game plan. Now, he was in the process of gauging something altogether different—namely whatever had prompted her mood earlier on.

'You can move in as quickly as next month, but it will entail quitting your job. I can't see the commute working.'

'Mateo…'

'If you want to hang on at the school, then be my guest, but the seller wants to get rid of the house as soon as possible and there are already three offers under review. I'll outstrip them all, but only on your say so.'

'Can I think about it?'

Mateo shrugged. 'I'd say you have little more than twenty-four hours to do that.'

'I'm just so attached to the school and to all my friends there.'

Mateo gritted his teeth and tried to check resurfacing notions of some fellow teacher laying it on thick about Alice's situation, mopping up her tears of sadness that she hadn't found true love with the father of her baby. Jealousy didn't usually feature in his life but he was having a hard time fighting it. When he thought of her pouring out her disappointment to some other guy, he literally saw red.

'What was all that about?' he ground out, before clearing his throat and trying to sound as composed as possible, given the weird feelings tearing through him.

'What was all what about?'

'Your mood earlier on.'

'I…'

'Don't be shy—it's not your style. I'm too accustomed to you saying exactly what you think so, like I said, spit it out.'

'If you must know, I saw a picture of you—actually, several pictures of you.'

'No idea what you're talking about.'

'I happened to be looking through the paper in the staff room and there you were, at some do or other last week, with a blonde.'

'Ah. I see.' He did see, quite a bit. In a heartbeat he thought…to heck with the long game. He should never have denied the man he was, the guy who'd literally fought to get where he was, the guy who'd always known that all was fair in love and war. 'I think I remember the occasion—a bash for a charity dealing with mental health issues in youngsters.'

'And was the woman with you?'

'That's not really your concern, now, is it, Alice?'

Had there been a blonde woman there? More than likely. Expensive charity fund raisers with high-profile guests usually attracted a very pretty crowd, and a lot of them tended to gravitate towards him.

'No, I know that. I was just a little curious, that's all.'

'But curiosity about who I may or may not be going out with doesn't enter the equation, not now.' He slowed down and pulled into one of the spaces close to the restaurant and waited for her to digest what he had just said for a few minutes, then he opened the door for her, and they walked to the place he had booked for them.

'If you had chosen to accept my marriage proposal,' he told her as soon as they were seated and water had been poured, 'then you would naturally have had a right to that kind of curiosity, but you chose another road, and that road has a different set of rules.'

'Forget I asked.'

'No, I won't. You *did* ask and now's a good time for us to discuss this. If I happened to have gone to that bash with a woman, then I don't have to answer to you for that decision, because what we have here, right now, is something that exists purely for the sake of the baby inside you. I want you to look a little into the future when our baby starts growing up and I want you to get used to the idea that there will be women in my life and then, eventually, just the one woman, because as a father I will no longer be interested in playing the field.'

'I've already thought about that, Mateo.'

Mateo chose to ignore her because some keen sixth sense had picked up a thread in her reaction that was the very same thing that had been bothering him. The tone of her voice when she'd asked about the woman at the party had given a lot away and he intended to use that to his advantage.

She wanted love, but she didn't want *him* to find it. She would have been happy for him to remain celi-

bate in the background, even though she would real-
istically know that that was never going to happen. If
she'd thought about him moving on, then it had been in
an abstract way. until now…

'And that may happen sooner rather than later,' he told
her gravely. 'I take my responsibilities seriously, and a
woman by my side is something I would find desirable.'

'That's so different from what you said when I first
told you that I was pregnant.'

'I… I had my reasons for being wary of jumping
into marriage because of a pregnancy,' Mateo said with
driven honesty. He raked his fingers through his hair
and looked at her, jaw clenched as memories took over.

It was so rare for him to lose control of the narrative
when it came to his private life that he floundered and
only picked back up the thread after a few seconds of
silence. She wasn't urging him to open up and he appreciated that.

'When I rushed into marriage with Bianca, it was
because she was pregnant. It was early days, but I was
keen to do the right thing, even though we'd been on the
point of breaking up. It was a mistake. Bianca miscar-
ried three weeks after we married, but we were locked
into a situation by then that was never going to work
out. I gave it my best shot but it was a harsh lesson in
how the head should always rule the heart. If I'd used
my head, I would have worked out that our relationship
was fundamentally flawed and would never have sur-
vived even if a child had been involved.'

'I'm really sorry, Mateo. That must have been such
a painful time for you.'

'Life happens. We divorced.'

'But you should never have married,' Alice said slowly. 'And then along I come, telling you that I'm pregnant, and of course you don't want to repeat your mistake. So why the change of heart?'

'The minute I saw our baby on that scan, something kicked in,' Mateo admitted truthfully, in a rough undertone. 'It was different with Bianca. I was very young, and the baby was more of an abstract reality, but seeing that baby move...the heartbeat.'

He glanced away and clenched his jaw. 'So here we are,' he continued in a cool, measured voice. 'I will meet someone, Alice. I will marry. My first choice would be to marry the mother of my child, but failing that I will not remain a bachelor playing Dad from a distance. If you want the cottage, I intend to have a place of my own also in Richmond, which I will share with the woman I make my wife, and there will be more than just the two of us then in the family unit. So the blonde lady? I may have a little fun for a while, but not for long, I predict.'

He looked at her and then said, without bothering to beat around the bush, 'You don't like the thought of me having another woman dangling from my arm, do you?'

'It's not that. I wouldn't want any child of ours to be exposed to a dad who plays the field.'

'Which, I assure you, I won't be doing by the time any child of ours is old enough to cotton on to anything like that. So I'll ask you one more time and then the question will no longer be posed—do you want to finally accept the benefits of marrying me, or are you aiming for the blended family, because you still think that love is really the one and only thing that matters here?

'I'll repeat for your benefit: Bianca and I were a mistake before we tied the knot. You and I? We're not. This chemistry between us… We can be lovers again and, if we're both honest to ourselves, isn't that what we want? Tie this knot, Alice, and it remains tied. You'll never open a sordid magazine to find me pictured with a blonde on my arm again, ever. Your choice.'

CHAPTER EIGHT

ALICE HAD SAID YES: that had been seven weeks ago. Since then, things had moved fast. In two days' time, they would be moving into the house she had looked around. He'd seemed startled when she'd asked him, some time back, if it wouldn't be be too modest for his taste.

'We come from very different worlds, Mateo,' she had told him when she had accepted his marriage proposal. 'Whichever side of the tracks you've come from, you've ended up on the side where the pavements are lined with gold, and I'm not sure if you're going to find somewhere as unassuming as that cottage up to your current standards—especially if you'll be living there with me full-time, not visiting once a week from your über-modern mansion on Mount Olympus.'

He'd grinned. 'I'll prove you wrong,' he'd asserted, with such ease that she had been reassured and surprised at the same time. But, sure enough, he hadn't looked back.

He had left the bulk of the soft-furnishing shopping to her, and had got a heavy-duty team of contractors on board, who had set to work turning one old and slightly dilapidated Victorian house into a work of art, while keeping every single original feature intact. It had been done at speed because no expense had been spared.

The wedding date had been set: a quiet affair with just close family and friends, to be held at the very parish church where her father preached. The small village was abuzz with excitement and her mother had swooped in with commendable enthusiasm for every part of the process, from picking out flowers to organising the choir.

Amidst all this, she expanded as the baby had grown, and there was not a single moment when she didn't feel Mateo's deep and honest involvement with the tiny human being maturing inside her. But he would never love her; of that she was now sure, having heard the rest of his story when it came to marriage and, as it turned out, pregnancy.

Everything about his relationship with his ex-wife explained the man Mateo was now. Not only had he rushed into marriage way too young but the marriage had been propelled by a pregnancy neither he nor his young girlfriend had planned.

However hardened he had been back then, he had obviously still been romantic enough to hope for a positive outcome. Maybe he had secretly thought that whatever love they'd shared at the start could be resurrected with a baby on the way. But the evolution of that relationship—the divorce, then the woman returning years later to try and fleece him for money—had opened his eyes to the bitter fact that not only had that love been little more than an illusion, but the very business of opening himself up a fraction could be disastrous.

Roll the clock on and Alice knew that, while she might love Mateo, he would only ever return love with, at best, affection mingled with a sense of duty. He wasn't a guy who ignored learning curves and he had had his fill of them.

But she had had a glimpse of what her life would be like if she let him go. Forget all her high-minded principles of not wanting to suffer the pain of being with a guy who didn't love her. The truth was that seeing him with that blonde woman had shown her that the pain of actually seeing him move on would always be hard for her to bear.

She would just have to plaster a smile on her face when she was with him, always keep a careful guard on her emotions and love him from afar, knowing that to be open about how she felt would risk turning him off.

And who knew? There were always surprises round every corner. He might not come to love her in the way that *she* defined love, but he could come to *need* her, and that would be a step up from affection.

Want and need were close companions, weren't they? And he wanted her. It was there every time he glanced at her, or looked at her until her body was raging with an urgent, primal burn. One that matched his. Oh, how glorious it was to be able to feel that hard, perfect body once again.

She'd made her choice at his ultimatum: marriage and the knot tied for good, lovers once again. Since then, permission granted, they had fallen back into each other's arms with the exquisite satisfaction of two people who knew each other intimately, who revelled in the pleasure of touching.

There was no question how he felt for her on a physical level: he wanted her. Honestly, whatever doubts she might harbour about this situation, one thing was absolutely clear: this part of their relationship worked and who knew if this one thing might not grow into more? One day he might need her. *Need* would make it harder for him to stray when the physicality between them eased away and he no longer wanted to touch her the way he wanted to touch her now.

Right now, getting done the final touches before she left for the leaving party her friends at the school were throwing for her, Alice blushed at the thought of those touches, that *physicality*. *She* would never tire of the way he could make her body sing and even now, with it swelling and getting bigger, he was still turned on—more so, if anything.

She didn't get it. When she thought of that woman she'd seen in the picture, leggy, skinny and tall enough to look Mateo in the eye instead of roughly somewhere in the region of his chest, Alice could only wince at the unfavourable comparison. She knew that she was marrying the most gorgeous, eligible bachelor on the planet through default and she had to fight to overcome the occasional burst of insecurity that generated in her. Yet, when he traced the contours of her swollen belly with such tenderness, she had no doubt that he wasn't put off by her expanding girth.

Sometimes, at night, she wondered how things might change after the baby was born, which was no longer in the distant future. Would the romance of an unborn child and the adventure that represented turn into the more prosaic business of sleepless nights and exhausted days? Would he still be turned on by a tired, yawning wife who didn't have time to look after herself because of the demands of an infant? Would temptation elsewhere begin to beckon as the mysterious pull of her pregnant body no longer existed?

Since she had no answers to those questions, and since she knew that speculation would only end up with her in a place where she probably wouldn't want to be, Alice boxed up those concerns, to be considered some other time in the future.

She stepped back and looked at her reflection with a critical eye. She could see the change in her shape, the small but distinct roundness of her expanding belly. Possibly not a great idea to go for bright, summery colours when she was short, genetically plump and a few months' pregnant. But, then again, she looked cheerful, which was exactly how she felt as she saw the beep on her phone: Mateo's driver outside and waiting for her. She flew out, grabbing her bag and her lightweight jacket on the way.

She would miss her friends, but would still keep in touch with many of them socially, and, if she was finishing a tiny bit ahead of the usual maternity-leave schedule then that was fine. Deep down, she could see the sense of taking it easy and relaxing before the baby came along rather than trying to prove a point about independence when she really didn't need to work. She would enjoy herself and then look forward to the new chapter in her life in a couple of days, when they moved in to their new place together.

Right now, she was still in the rented apartment Mateo had moved her to and Mateo had said he was making sure that as many complex deals were completed as possible before the baby came along. Alice hadn't protested and, while she trusted him, she knew that there was no such thing as certainties in life, so she made damn sure not to go near any gossip pages just in case.

But tonight wasn't for any anxious thoughts. Tonight was for enjoying herself.

Mateo had no idea why he had decided to surprise Alice at the school where her leaving do was being held. Things were exactly as he had hoped for: she had accepted his marriage proposal.

He was guiltily aware that a certain amount of tactical economy with the truth had played into that decision. He'd painted a nicely vivid picture of what Alice could expect when he found another woman. He'd allowed her to think that, having had his proposal turned down, he was already easing himself back into the dating scene...even though he hadn't looked in the direction of another woman since Alice had returned to his life. But he had no regrets about those creative liberties. He'd got what he'd wanted and it was for the best.

What could beat two parents united and together when it came to bringing up the child they shared? What could beat the fire between them? He'd resisted her for as long as he could when he'd been waiting for her to come to him, but he had prodded and she had come to him, and it was damn near wonderful not having to deny what his body wanted—what both their bodies wanted!

There was no way she could deny that they got along. He'd been nothing but accommodating—the ideal husband to be and father in the making. But he was beginning to think that proving himself was a vain pursuit, because she honestly didn't seem to notice all his hard work.

For instance, she had no idea how much grit it had taken to accept the wedding taking place in weeks rather than hours. He had nodded, murmured something or other and battled the instinct that had pushed him to firm things up while he still had her, because the longer they delayed walking down the aisle the more time it allowed her to reconsider.

For the guy who'd never given marriage a second's thought in years, he found himself in the challenging position of desperately wanting it now.

He hadn't raised an eyebrow when she'd made noises about the house he'd bought being too modest for his taste. True, he would have gravitated to something bigger and more impersonal, but he'd been quick to appreciate that that would never have been to her taste. Besides, as she had pointed out, infants were allergic to too much white and too many hard edges. So he'd left the choice of whatever décor she wanted to her.

He'd likewise listened with interest as she'd rambled on about resuming work locally once the baby was born. He didn't see the point of that, but he was determined to prove to her that she hadn't made a mistake when it came to giving in to him and giving up on whatever romantic dreams she still clung to.

Yet, he had caught glimpses of her when she hadn't realised he'd been watching her and her expression had hardly been one of undiluted joy. At times like that, his gut instinct was to touch her, because on that one front he was perfectly secure.

Her body curved to his as natural as a flower keening towards the sun, but he had to resist that because it was a cheap fix; he knew that. They could still lose themselves when they were making love, get to a place where nothing mattered and there was no sadness, thoughtfulness or anything at all but enjoyment of the moment, but more and more he found that he wanted more than just passing enjoyment.

He wanted her to smile *all the time*. He just didn't know how to get there with that.

So he'd decided that he'd surprise her at her staff party—maybe remind her somehow that he was there for her and the baby. Show her that the life she was leaving behind wasn't one that she should file under the heading of 'whimsical nostalgia for the good times'. If she conditioned herself to think of her past as a sacrifice she'd been obliged to make, then there would be no chance of her ever really accepting the present without wondering whether an alternative would have been better.

He could have told her to expect him but he favoured the element of surprise. It was only as his driver neared the uninspiring building that he realised something: part of him was curious to see her in her natural habitat rather than his.

He knew the code to the door. With the agreement of the other members of staff, she had been allowed to share it with him. Mateo thought that his hefty financial contribution to the school finances might also have had a little something to do with that particular decision, but had tactfully refrained from pointing that out. Time had shown him that she was naive when it came to her accepting the unpalatable truth that money bought pretty much everyone and everything. Probably because she was the one exception to that rule.

He'd been to the school on a number of occasions and knew the layout pretty well, although it felt a little eerie to wander around without the noise of kids everywhere. Lord only knew why they'd chosen to have a party at the school, but Alice had been thrilled. She'd wanted it to be informal and private. And besides, she had confided at the time, her memories were all there, which was important to her. She hadn't wanted lots of waiters and staff faffing around, serving them, with a deadline for them to leave and no music allowed.

He followed the noise. Only essential lighting was on in the corridors and the doors to the classrooms were all firmly shut. It wasn't a big school, serving kids between the ages of eleven and sixteen, with a sixth-form college standing on other grounds not far away. If he'd somehow looked at it through rose-tinted specs, he would say that it was as cosy as a functional, unimaginative concrete and glass block could possibly get. That was thanks to sheer ingenuity when it came to filling the unappealing wall space with posters.

Mateo heard old-school 80s music as he nudged open

the door to the staffroom, which was adorned with balloons, a banner and a long table groaning under the weight of food ordered in for the occasion.

And there she was: Alice.

She was chatting in a group, jigging about merrily and laughing.

Mateo drew in a sharp breath and remained standing where he was, framed in the doorway but not immediately noticeable in the dim room crowded with so many people—a huge turn-out for a popular teacher.

The door was angled in such a way that someone would have had to twist round to make him out, and no one was doing that. Everyone was too busy having a blast. At least thirty-five people were there. Most were dancing and there was a lot of laughter, talking and screeching.

Watching, Mateo felt as though he'd been hit in the chest with a sledgehammer, because what he saw on Alice's face was absolute joy, and that absolute joy was something he hadn't seen for a long time. He'd seen abandon when they'd made love, and appreciation for his thoughtfulness when they'd gone out for meals or visited the house they'd be sharing.

But that *absolute joy*? No.

He pushed himself into the room, feeling as out of place as he'd felt in a long time. She instantly spotted him.

In the middle of turning to fetch herself some more of the nibbles on the table, Alice stilled. The last person she had been expecting to see was Mateo.

She'd become so used to guarding her feelings around him, hiding her love because she knew that it wasn't returned, because she wanted to protect herself as much as she could. She stole glances at him when he wasn't looking, like a thief stealing a cache of gold to be inspected later in privacy, but she made sure to school her expression when she was with him. She couldn't let all her defences slip. Where would that leave her? As helpless as a turtle deprived of its protective shell.

He'd asked very few questions about the leaving party and she'd got the impression that he hadn't been all that interested. Why should he have been? she'd asked herself impatiently. The leaving party didn't involve the baby. The leaving party involved *her* and he wasn't interested enough in her to ask for details.

He came alive when he touched her, and his eyes lit up whenever they rested on her swollen stomach, proof positive that it was the baby he wanted. But otherwise he was kind, unfailingly attentive but keen on keeping some distance. Physical distance…no. Emotional distance…yes.

At least, that was what it felt like to Alice.

She drank the remainder of her lemonade, knowing that he'd been spotted from the awed reaction from everyone, and walked towards him. The conversation which had stopped for a few seconds picked back up again around her as she propelled her way forwards.

'What are you doing here?' was the first thing she asked when she was standing in front of him. 'I thought you said that you were going to be working late this evening.'

'Thought I'd surprise you, join in the fun. Are you disappointed that I've come?'

Alice hesitated. Disappointed? How could she ever be disappointed to see Mateo? He thrilled her to the bone. He looked sexy as hell, indolently leaning against the door frame, staring down at her in ways that made her whole body feel as though its primary mission in life was to fire up in readiness for him.

It was such a frustrating reaction that she reddened and scowled. 'Surprised. Come on through.'

She began turning away, but then saw that he wasn't immediately following suit, so she reluctantly turned back round to look at him.

'Wait. I... I don't want to interrupt your good time, Alice.'

'Why did you come, Mateo?'

'I came because...'

'Did you want to see how the other half live?'

'Of course not,' he said shortly.

'There are no waiters and waitresses here with great platters of expensive food and there's no champagne. Everyone put money into a kitty towards the food. Sarah, the dinner lady, did the spread. And we all brought some alcohol and soft drinks, and James is the DJ for the evening.'

'Why are you getting hot under the collar? Have I said anything about coming here because I wanted to see *how the other half live*?'

'No, but you weren't exactly very interested when I told you about this leaving do.'

Alice heard the hurt petulance in her voice with dismay. She was punishing him for not taking the sort of interest in her that she wanted him to, seeing his surprise arrival here as patronising rather than interested, and she was ashamed of the pettiness.

So far she hadn't involved herself in his social life, although in fairness he had invited her to an opening only a week before. Mateo might have come from a rough background, might have had to fight tooth and nail to get where he had, but now that he'd got there he blended in with the highest echelons of society as though he'd always belonged there. He knew how to do that because he didn't care.

Hormones suddenly seemed to surge through her. In a rush, she felt self-pity for having fallen for a guy who didn't return her love, and for her own blasted body, which reacted to him mindlessly every time he was within a metre of her. It all seemed hopeless as she stared down the barrel of a future of want, need and love, too much for her to contain but with nowhere to go.

She thought of how her life was going to change and it was really the first time she had given this thought house room. She would no longer have this cheerful crowd of friends around her every day. She would be mixing in a world that was going to be very different, and she had a moment of panic that she was just never going to be able to fit in.

'You shouldn't have come here,' she said sharply. Her hazel eyes flashed with misplaced anger as she stared up at his beautiful face, noting the way the shutters dropped.

'I wouldn't have,' Mateo returned tightly, 'if I'd known that the reception was going to be as hostile as it is. Why's that?'

Alice was steaming full ahead. Maybe it was just the fact of seeing him here, on the last day of life as she'd known it. She didn't know. She just knew that everything seemed to have piled up on top of her and this was where it burst its banks.

She glared at him, and in return he raised cool eyebrows and stared right back at her with unflinching aloofness.

'You don't get it!' she snapped miserably, half-stepping out of the room and then drawing the door behind them so that the world wasn't witnessing this stupid spat that had sprung from thin air.

'Tell me what I don't get.'

'I feel…' Alice left the sentence hanging in mid-air because she wasn't quite sure what she did feel. Things were not ideal but she thought she'd reasoned her way past the business of being in a loveless marriage. She knew that it was the right thing to do. So why all of a sudden was she miserable and tearful?

Was it because he had showed up here unannounced? Was he a reminder of the world she'd be entering in stark contrast to the one she would be leaving behind? Was there a part of her that was just pretending to accept the situation because she was afraid of the alternative? It felt unfair that love could be so painful.

She looked at him in mute, misplaced anger and then glanced down.

'Talk to me, Alice.'

He put one hand on her chin and tilted her face to his. When their eyes met, his were gentle and curious, which actually didn't make her feel much better.

'I don't want to talk,' she said with a defensive toss of her head.

'What do you want to do?'

'I'd quite like to make love to you.'

She watched the way his eyes darkened and the flush of simmering heat that stole into his face.

She didn't want *polite* and if this was the only way to get *passion* then, right now, it was a ploy she wasn't averse to using.

'I don't think an empty hall outside a staff room where there are forty people celebrating your immi- nent departure is going to do the trick, do you, Alice?'

'We could leave.'

'No, we could not.'

'Don't you want me? Don't you want to make love to me?'

'Where the hell is all this coming from?'

Alice shrugged, dealt him a challenging, provoca- tive stare from under her lashes and felt a kick of power. However polite he might be in his role of perfect hus- band to be, nothing could hide the flare of passion he still seemed able to provoke. How much longer that would last, she had no idea, and she knew that this un- certainty was just something else that unsettled her.

She sighed and looked at him ruefully.

'I'm just kidding,' she said. 'Come on through. It's fun in there. Everybody's really put themselves out and you know they all like you.'

'It was a mistake coming here,' Mateo returned roughly. 'But it's obvious something's on your mind and I want to know what that something is. I'll wait up for you.'

'You'll wait up for me?'

'I'll be at your place and, Alice…don't overdo it tonight.'

'Because I'm pregnant?' she couldn't help but ask sweetly, immediately spotting his area of concern which, of course was for the precious cargo she carried. 'Staying up late isn't going to damage the baby, Mateo. I'm pregnant. I'm not ill!'

He didn't say anything. He gave her one final look before turning on his heel and walking away and she followed him with her eyes until the door had shut behind him.

Mateo was sprawled on the sofa in Alice's apartment and was consulting his watch for the eighth time in less than an hour when he heard the sound of her key being inserted in the door.

He'd left her over three hours ago. It had been a mistake to surprise her at her leaving do. He hadn't been invited for a reason, and the reason had become patently obvious the second she had spotted him. He'd seen the dismay on her face, noted the way the laughter had died on her lips and had known that she hadn't asked him along because she hadn't wanted him there.

He'd never been in a position like that in his life but Mateo was already growing accustomed to the fact that there was a Mateo that had existed before Alice and one that existed post-Alice. The post-Alice version could take nothing for granted and was conscious of the fact that at any given moment he might find himself in alien territory without any signposts and no idea what lay round the corner.

He certainly hadn't foreseen being dismissed in not so many words. As soon as he had walked out of the building, his imagination had gone into overdrive. He'd remembered the happiness on her face before she'd spotted him and then he'd tried to think who she'd been with in that little group.

Had there been any men there? Mateo had always prided himself on not being jealous. In fact, he'd never cared about his girlfriend's exes and had never had the slightest concern about any of them playing the field behind his back. Why should he? Few could match what he brought to the table and the women he dated had always been grateful to go out with him. He'd grown lazy, it had to be said, and Alice never failed to remind him of that.

But as he waited for her, nursing one drink for the entire time and unable to focus on anything but the crazy scenarios in his head, he did his best to try and recall who'd been there.

Had she been having a few last flirtatious encounters for the road? She was pregnant, for God's sake! Mateo didn't know where his runaway brain was going with that scenario but, once it took root, it refused to budge.

Was there some teacher there who had had a crush on her before the whole pregnancy thing had happened? Before she had found herself in the position of having to seek him out through sheer decency, only to find herself embroiled with him because he'd given her as little choice as he could get away with? Because he had played on her driving need to do the right thing?

Was that a great place for him to be? Since when had a ruthless need to get what he wanted trumped generosity of spirit?

Maybe the time for talking had finally come—and this time he would have to accept whatever outcome it led to.

CHAPTER NINE

MATEO VAULTED UPRIGHT as soon as Alice was through the door. She looked surprised to see him, even though he'd warned her that he'd be waiting for her in her apartment.

'You're here,' she said, walking through and dumping her bag on the table, along with a sack of unopened presents wrapped in brightly coloured paper.

'I told you I would be.'

'Mateo, I'm honestly not in the mood to talk.'

'Was it a good leaving do?'

'The best.' She sighed. 'You shouldn't have waited up for me, Mateo. I'm dead on my feet.'

Mateo watched her as she struggled out of her lightweight coat and kicked off her shoes.

He looked at her stomach and gritted his teeth in frustration at the sudden disarray of their carefully formed plan. He knew that he should back off but he'd hated to do it. He didn't want to stress her out but he was breaking up inside.

'I expected you back a little earlier than...' he made a show of consulting his watch '...nearly twelve-thirty.'

'You're not my gatekeeper, Mateo—plus twelve-thirty is hardly the early hours of the morning. We were all having fun; we started playing games at eleven, and it was so riotous that the time just flew past.'

She was still in a mood and that cut him to the quick. He didn't understand. Where did they go from here? How long was she going to be in a mood? Was it hormone-driven—understandable nerves as the due date galloped towards them? Or cold feet before a wedding she hadn't wanted in the first place? It didn't pay to forget that she had already been engaged once and had broken off that engagement... He wasn't the only one with a back story.

Suddenly, the conversation staring him in the face felt bigger than before. He'd barely asked her about that broken engagement. She had mentioned it in passing the very first time they had met, and had vaguely brushed it off as the reason she had fled her friends and taken to dangerous slopes in that fast-gathering blizzard that had thrown them together.

Now it felt imperative that he find out what happened there. Could history be about to repeat itself? Mateo suddenly felt sick with panic.

The baby; this was all about the baby and the fact that he wanted what was best for their child, wasn't it? This was his highly developed sense of responsibility kicking in and he would have it no other way. He was sure of that.

Sudden uncertainty drove him towards her. He moved to reach out, felt her stiffen for a few seconds and then the predictable melting of her body as it reacted to his.

'Remember you told me that you wanted me...?'

* * *

Alice buried her head into his chest. He hadn't changed. He kept a stash of clothes at the apartment, as she did at his, but he was still in the trousers he had showed up in and his white shirt, which was rolled to the cuffs, although the hand-made Italian shoes were off and he was barefoot. It was a breathtakingly sexy combination at nearly one in the morning, she couldn't help but think.

She felt her belly pushing against him and felt her clothes a barrier between them although, as her body surged into shameful life, it was a barrier she didn't think was going to be there for much longer. Jeez, was it always going to be like this—one touch and all self-control down the drain?

She moaned softly as he slid his hand along her back; there was no zip. The dress was softly stretchy and very easy for him to ease up, scraping it against her thighs and then over her stomach until he could flip it over her head with a bit of help from her eager, scrabbling hands.

He stood back and looked at her. The lighting was subdued. He'd been lounging in semi-darkness while he'd waited for her.

'Take the bra off,' he commanded shakily, and Alice was only too happy to oblige, reaching round to unhook it and then sighing as she was freed of the constraint. She'd always been generously endowed, and her breasts had gone up a size since the pregnancy.

'God, you're beautiful,' Mateo said in a strangled voice and he moved to her, gently guiding her to the sofa as though actually reaching the bedroom hadn't even been a consideration.

Alice subsided onto the sofa, which was huge and very comfortable. 'The bed would be a whole lot more comfortable,' she murmured.

'Ah, but starters can be served here, my darling...'

Alice smiled. She knew his touches so well and yet every time they made love it felt new, wonderful and special.

He knelt at the side of the sofa and she twisted so that she was lying on her side, making it easy for him to nibble at her breast, and then separate them with his hand to suckle gently on her nipple, which had darkened and grown, and was so sensitive that the slightest lick was enough very nearly to take her over the edge.

He knew that and continued to torment her with his tongue, which flicked darts of exquisite sensation through her. His hand on her belly was tender and gentle, as were his lips, and then, moving between her legs, the idle flick of his tongue slipped into her wetness and drove her insane.

He knew how to make her forget everything but the moment, and Alice barely realised when they left the sofa and made it into the bedroom. She was so conscious of the weight she'd gained, maybe because she hadn't been a slip of a thing in the first place, but Mateo was still strong enough to sweep her off her feet and carry her through to the bedroom as though she weighed nothing.

The love-making was slow and gentle. He touched her as though she were as delicate as a piece of porcelain, despite her constantly telling him that she was actually as strong as an ox. Deep down, she couldn't deny the lovely feeling of feminine helplessness at his protectiveness. It was just one more thing to add to the list of reasons for loving him.

Would that all disappear once the baby was born and he was no longer bothered about her fragile status? The disturbing thought drifted through her head, but she pushed it away, and then it was easy to do what she always did and sink into his caresses, letting her body get carried away on a tide of love, passion and fulfilment.

Her body was tingling all over, über-sensitive and on fire, when she finally climaxed, arching up against him and wrapping her arms around his neck so that she could pull him towards her, losing herself in him.

'Now I really am tired…' She yawned, stretching out and then squinting as he slid off her and lay flat on his back with one arm flung over his eyes.

'It was unfair of me to distract you when it was already so late.'

'You didn't do anything I didn't want to do, trust me.' Alice laughed and curved onto her side to look at him.

'Get some sleep, Alice.'

'You too.' She peered at him, although her eyelids were already beginning to feel heavy as she reached for her underwear on the ground and then smiled as he brought her the baggy tee she was accustomed to sleeping in. 'You wanted to talk?' she said reluctantly.

'It can wait. I'm going to try and get some work done. I'll make sure I don't wake you when I come to bed…'

Mateo nudged open the bedroom door at just after eight the following morning. She'd been sound asleep when he'd finally joined her in the early hours of the morning, snoring gently and curled on her side, wrapped around a pillow which supported her bump. They'd made love and, for a while, he'd forgotten the unsettling feelings he had had when he'd surprised her at the leaving party. Making love tended to do that. Unfortunately, uncomfortable notions could only be pushed to the side for so long before they popped back up, demanding to be acknowledged.

He had made her breakfast. It was something he had never done for a woman before, but he needed to clear the air, and getting her onside with some toast and coffee didn't seem too big an ask.

'Surprise,' he announced, dropping the tray deftly on the table next to the bed and then straightening to look at her as she shifted into an awkward sitting position with the pillows propped behind her.

She was pink and ruffled, her long hair a chaotic tangle that somehow made her look a lot younger than she was, a mere girl instead of a woman on the brink of having a baby.

'You should have woken me, Mateo. I know it's the weekend but, now that I won't have a job to wake up for on Monday, I don't want to get into the habit of just lazing around in bed until mid-morning.'

Mateo smiled. 'You happen to have a very good excuse.' He poured her some coffee and handed her the cup, then he arranged the tray to the side of her and pulled up a chair next to the bed. 'Besides, from tomorrow, you're going to be busy with the house move.'

Mention of the house they would be moving to was

a reminder of a conversation that needed to be had. But now he found that he was happy to put it off, happy not to hear her tell him that this wasn't the life she had banked on.

He'd got his own way with the marriage but it seemed that there was more to life than getting his own way.

'Delicious toast, Mateo.'

'I'll make sure to contact the bakery to congratulate them on the quality of the bread. I'm sorry I showed up last night, Alice. I…hadn't meant to. It was something of a spur-of-the-moment decision.'

'It's okay.' Alice reddened.

'Want to know *why* I decided to unexpectedly show up?'

'Yes,' Alice said cautiously. 'Maybe.'

'It's a big step—moving in together, getting married. And it may have seemed more distant, when these things were agreed between us, but time's moving on. House move next week and then, before you know it, we're married and a new chapter begins.'

Working her way through the toast, Alice looked at Mateo warily from under her lashes. 'What does that have to do with you turning up at my leaving party?' she asked with genuine curiosity.

She felt at a distinct disadvantage. She knew that she was rumpled from having just woken up, and her baggy tee-shirt wasn't exactly the sort of power outfit required for a conversation that sounded serious.

He, on the other hand, looked bright-eyed and bushy-tailed in black jeans and a black jumper that fitted him like a glove. Nerves slammed into her and all of a sudden the toast tasted like cardboard.

'I think I ought to get dressed,' she said, clearing her throat. 'I don't think that a bed is the right place for us to be having a serious conversation.'

'Okay. I'll wait for you in the living room. Want some more coffee?'

He was already standing as she shook her head and pushed back the duvet. She felt a vice-like grip around her heart. So it was going to be a serious conversation. How much more serious did conversations get than ones that included a marriage proposal—except, perhaps, one where it was retracted?

She waited till he had left the bedroom then had a quick shower and dressed hurriedly in loose jogging bottoms and a loose top, stuff she could move around in, because anything with a waistband was out of the question.

He had deposited a pile of money in an account for her but so far she had bought nothing for herself with any of it, despite his gentle reminders that it wasn't there to gather cobwebs.

'I've got things for the baby,' she'd replied vaguely.

He'd laughed and said, 'The money is for you as well. You're going to be my wife. You'll need a wardrobe of clothes that aren't just serviceable, Alice. Feel free to buy whatever designer things you want, and that includes whatever designer things you find to accommodate your beautiful, growing shape.'

'That's a waste,' she'd responded politely, reminded of the new role her brand new life was going to entail as wife of a billionaire, 'When they'll only get used for a matter of a few weeks.'

She emerged into the beautiful, spacious sitting room with an air of quiet defiance.

He was waiting for her. The apartment was completely open-plan with only the bedroom and the bathroom enclosed. Unlike Mateo's own enormous house, this apartment was modern but informal. It had come furnished with comfortable sofas, and the wooden floor was scuffed but gleaming, proud testimony to all the people who had enjoyed the space.

Alice paused and looked at him for a few seconds, trying to decipher what was going through his head from the thoughtful expression on his face. His beauty never failed to shock her. Maybe that, along with everything else, had piled up on top of her recently, making her pensive and cautious around him.

Had he picked up on that? Was that the reason for his sudden urge to have a serious conversation with her? They'd made love but he hadn't forgotten that he still wanted to talk to her. Making love wasn't a panacea that encouraged forgetfulness, not in this instance.

She took a deep breath and joined him, curling up on the sofa next to him and laboriously positioning herself so that she was looking straight at him; he, in turn, did the same.

'Why am I nervous?' she opened with a little laugh.

'Are you?'

'You're sitting there as though you're about to interview me for a position in your company.'

Mateo laughed. 'I'm struggling to think of anyone

who might be less interested in working in my company. Since when have you expressed any interest in the nuts and bolts of what I do?'

'It's not because I'm not interested.'

'Yes, it is, and I like that. I can't think of anything more boring than coming home to a wife who wants the details of what deals I managed to put away.'

Heartened by that, Alice smiled and relaxed.

'I suppose,' Mateo said thoughtfully, 'as the time goes on I'm curious about…well, to name but one thing… your broken engagement. You haven't told me a huge amount about that, about what happened there. You've mentioned it in passing, and I've let it go, but now…tell me what happened?'

Something must have occurred to him and he frowned. 'I've never been a guy who believes in a lot of hand-holding and confidence sharing, but it's suddenly occurring to me that I've shared a lot more with you than you have with me.'

It was an uncomfortable realisation and he flushed darkly and shot her a fulminating, vaguely accusatory look from under his lashes.

'So?' he prompted.

'So it just didn't work out. It wasn't that it ended on a bad note. In fact, I can't really recall what sort of note it ended on—an amicable one. Which is probably why, when I told you about him, told you that it was all very friendly in the end, you immediately concluded that he must have been boring.'

'Did I conclude that?'

Alice shrugged and smiled. 'You did. "Nice but dull"

was the way you summed him up when I told you that I'd ended the relationship.' She frowned. 'If you want to know, it was something I sleep-walked into. At least, that's what it feels like looking back. I was young and we were good together: friendly; no highs and no lows... We got along, and I suppose I never thought I'd do anything but end up with a nice guy in a solid relationship and Simon seemed to fit the bill. You were right, though. He wasn't for me. I didn't analyse at the time what I wanted but I just knew that I wanted more. All history.' She shrugged.

'I surprised you at your leaving party because I wanted to see you in your own comfort zone.' Mateo abruptly changed the subject and Alice looked at him, startled at this admission.

'And? You surprised me but then you didn't join the party. Everyone wanted to know what happened to you, why you showed up and then just disappeared.'

'What did you tell them?'

'That something had come up with the house. You had to make a decision about something and needed my input but you couldn't get through to me on my mobile and you were in the area.'

'And they fell for that?'

'They were too busy having fun to go into a question-and-answer session.'

'And you were as well.'

'Meaning?'

Alice felt that they were going round in circles and, because she knew that Mateo was a direct person who couldn't be bothered with conversational niceties, she couldn't stop a tremor of nerves.

He'd implied that they were still going to be married. It was crazy but, having dug her heels in to start with at the whole marriage idea, she had given in the minute she had seen that picture of him with another woman. It was as though the reality of an alternative situation had hit her hard enough for her to put things in perspective. She had accepted his proposal even as she'd accepted that it wasn't ideal and had told herself that nothing in life was ideal. She'd kept her love guarded, but there had been a sadness behind the acceptance that it was a one-sided relationship and would probably always remain that way.

She knew that she'd been skittish around him recently, and she wondered whether he'd picked up on that. Uncertainty swooped through her, shaking her to the foundations. For good or bad, she knew that she *wanted* this man, *wanted* to be married to him and damn the consequences; she would live with them.

'Alice...' Mateo's voice was low and quiet. 'I looked at you at that party and you were laughing.'

'I was having a good time.'

'That's my point. What we have here...' He spread his arms wide to encompass the room they were in, the apartment, everything around them. He raked his fingers through his hair and vaulted upright to pace the room in restless, jerky strides while Alice remained where she was, following him with anxious eyes and wondering where this was going.

'What we have here is duty and obligation, based on

mutual respect and a healthy sex life as a foundation for a union.'

'There's nothing wrong with any of that. You yourself said so from the start!'

Her heart picked up speed. She wanted to spring to her feet and dash over to where he was still prowling the room so that she could hold onto him. But then would that just be taking refuge in physical contact again?

She looked down and clenched her hands into balls, willing him to just shut up and overlook whatever blip had recently happened between them instead of dragging it out into the open and analysing it. Since when had he been the guy who liked having heart-to-hearts? Couldn't he just do them both a favour right now and return to type, scorn this chat he insisted on having?

'And when I said that I meant it, but time has a habit of changing everything,' Mateo returned in a low, driven voice. 'I see now that, whilst I can be perfectly happy with those ingredients, unlike you I'm not the sentimental sort. You broke off your engagement with Simon because you wanted more than he could offer. Maybe he offered you the sort of neutral love that wasn't enough; you wanted more. The *more* you wanted then will always be the *more* you want now—the *more* that I can't give you. Alice, I saw you laughing with your friends. You don't laugh like that with me.'

Mateo's words hung in the air between them and there was nothing Alice could do to deny the truth in them. He was so right, because Simon had never been quite enough, had never offered the love her heart craved. He had never been anywhere close to Mateo, this dif-

ficult, complex, proud, caring guy who had everything
she wanted but would never give it to her.

There was a reason she hadn't laughed in a while.
Laughter would come again but it had been in short sup-
ply as she had grappled with circumstances that gave
so much and withheld so much more. Grappled with a
union where the sex was so sweet and the caring nature
of Mateo so undisguised…and yet a union in which the
love she so desperately wanted, the love that only he
could give her, was not forthcoming. Putting her guard
up had made her cautious, and caution had kept that
open, honest laughter in check.

And then all sorts of other thoughts had swirled in
her head of late, exacerbated by hormones and sudden
apprehension at the future awaiting her.

Looking at the shadows flitting across her face, Mateo
almost cursed himself for having said anything. What
he had just said had made him sound vulnerable. He
wasn't the vulnerable sort, but the words were out there,
and he couldn't retract them. He didn't know whether
he even wanted to.

Just like that, clarity came to him with sudden, shock-
ing force.

A chance meeting: he'd opened his door to a woman
lost in a blizzard and he hadn't realised that, in doing
so, he had also opened the door to a world of emotion
he had thought to be beyond him.

As realisations struck him, he could do no more than
make for the nearest chair and sink into it. Frankly, if it

wasn't so early in the day, he would have been seriously tempted to see if a slug of whisky might not help things.

Suddenly released from their restraints, his thoughts ran rampant, coming at him from all directions as the silence built up between them. Snowbound on those slopes, he'd thought that he was enjoying was some harmless fun with a woman who was way too sexy to resist. He'd gone to his lodge to escape the frantic, high-voltage world that occupied him for fifty-one weeks of the year. He'd taken his usual week off to recharge his batteries and remind himself that, in life, it paid to remember your roots.

He'd gone for peace, solitude and some edge-of-his-seat skiing…and instead he'd found Alice. They'd lived in a bubble for a while, marooned in his lodge and discovering one another. What he'd thought was just going to be a week of unexpected fun had turned into something completely different, and just how different that something was now hit him with the force of a sledge-hammer.

He'd fallen in love with her. How and when, Mateo had no idea, but it was something that had crept up on him as stealthily as a thief in the night, overthrowing his defences and leaving him powerless.

They'd parted company, but how could he not have realised what had happened when he'd returned to London only to find his thoughts consumed with her? He knew now that if she hadn't contacted him he would eventually have been driven to seek her out. He might have used some feeble pretext or other, but he would have pursued her because he would have had to. Love would not have given him the option of remaining detached.

When she had showed up at his office out of the blue, he couldn't have foreseen how circumstances were going to change for him. Yet, even as he'd waded through the shock of her announcement, he had failed to feel anything but a certain gut deep pleasure at the thought of fatherhood suddenly thrust at him.

Why on earth hadn't he immediately insisted on marriage? He'd gone into a position of instant self-defence, holding himself back from the ultimate commitment, because he'd been there before and had arrogantly presumed to know that it might just be a case of making another mistake, of stepping into a raging fire, because of a pregnancy.

He'd let his past determine his present and he had paid a steep price—because here they were, and he knew that she was having second thoughts whether she said so or not. He'd seen her happy, had seen that look of joy on her face when she'd been surrounded by her friends and colleagues, and he knew that she was wondering what she was doing.

Would she actually say anything—express doubts? Probably not. She'd made up her mind and she would stick to doing what he had persuaded her was the right thing to do. She'd seen some stupid picture of him with a blonde, had been spooked and he'd used that as an opportunity to drive home to her what it would mean if she didn't marry him. She'd paid attention and gone against the grain. She'd given up her hopes of finding true love in favour of following his line of argument.

That his argument was valid didn't seem to matter to Mateo just at the moment. What mattered was that look of joy on her face—a look that would never be spared for him. He could give her the world, but it would never be enough because she didn't love him and, more than that, she wasn't impressed with his wealth.

He'd never been one for looking back over his shoulder at things that had come and gone. Lessons were learnt and time moved on. Now, though, he looked back and saw a life conditioned by his experience dealing with a father whose future had collapsed when his wife had died and who had needed propping up by a son too young for the task. He saw a life with his ex, a woman who had cared for money more than she had cared for him, and him being happy to go along with that because giving money had been a very different thing from giving his heart. He had given his heart to Alice and had fought tooth and nail to deny that because his drive to protect himself from hurt had been stronger than anything else. He couldn't do it. It was impossible. He could never let himself be vulnerable: down that road lay pain.

'Are you going to say anything?'

Mateo looked at her with a guarded expression. 'I'm going to say that I feel I've forced your hand when it comes to marrying me and there's still time for you to take a step back and really think about what you're letting yourself in for.' He shielded himself from the stab of pain that roared through his body like an arrow.

Alice felt the blood rush to her cheeks as she gazed in dismay at Mateo's serious face.

He was letting her go. One minute he'd wanted her, the next minute he didn't. It was as though their time-lines were all wrong. No sooner was she on his page than he was turning his back on that and moving on, and she was struggling to keep up.

But she couldn't pretend that he was wrong and that everything was just great. He would see through that in an instant, and she didn't want him to turn her away for her own good because he'd suddenly had an attack of conscience. This was a time when she should tell him how she felt, about her doubts, which were only to be expected. She would reassure him that things would work out, remind him of the bigger picture. She felt sick when she thought of him having second thoughts.

'I admit I've been feeling a little nervous recently,' she said on a deep breath. 'And I guess, when I was at the leaving party, it was all brought home to me.'

'Explain.'

'Everything…' Alice sighed. 'I was having fun, letting my hair down and when you showed up. I guess I saw what my old life looked like and what my new life was going to look like. But in all honesty it had hit me before that the world you live in is very different to mine. Remember I told you that, when you bought the cottage which would then become somewhere for both of us and the baby and not just me? Remember I told you that you might find it all a little cramped?'

'I remember,' Mateo said heavily.

'Mateo, I'm going to have to dress differently, go to things I've never gone to and present the sort of persona that will fit in with your lifestyle.'

'And of course, were we not to be married, that would not be a problem.'

'I suppose it wouldn't,' Alice agreed thoughtfully.

'No having to mix in my boring world,' Mateo said softly. 'No having to wear clothes you don't want to wear or make conversation with people you don't want to make conversation with. Would you prefer that?'

'I...'

'I know we've told everyone that we'll be getting married and things are in motion but...'

Mateo shook his head and glanced off into the distance. He'd tried. She'd wanted a relationship that had love at the centre of it rather than a baby, and he'd told her flat out that if she was looking for love, then he wasn't the guy who could give it to her—but, of course, she hadn't been looking for love with *him*.

His ego had been in the driving seat when he'd jumped to that conclusion. Seeing her letting her hair down, not wearing that wary look on her face that always seemed to be just there, just under the surface, ever since they had ironed out the whole marriage situation, had been the game changer.

If he loved someone, he shouldn't harness them to his side because of what *he* wanted. If he loved someone, he'd allow them to go to find their own destiny, even if he personally thought that their destiny was to be glued to his side.

Giving Alice the house of her dreams and more money than she could shake a stick at was never going to cut it, even if on paper it all made perfect sense, and even if he'd managed to get her round to his point of view that there was no viable alternative.

'I'm releasing you, Alice.'

'Sorry?'

'You don't have to go through with a marriage you originally had no interest in.'

He stood up but he couldn't meet her eyes. He didn't want her to see what was in his. Instead, he remained standing there in silence for a few seconds.

'I'll leave you to mull over what I've said. I want you to know that, aside from your freedom which I am returning to you, everything else will remain the same and that includes my unwavering commitment to you and to our child. I'll be with you every step of the way. You can count on me financially, and of course emotionally, until such time as you see fit.'

'Until such time as I see fit?'

'Correct.'

He began making for his coat and retrieving his mobile from where he had put in on the table in front of him, looking around vaguely as though he might have forgotten something.

Then he gave her a final look, brief and remote but not unkind.

'I'll be in touch. The move is in a couple of days. I'll be there to make sure everything goes smoothly— if, that is, you still want to live there and not closer to where your friends are?'

'And, if I went for the "closer to the friends" option, what would you do?'

Mateo shrugged. 'It wouldn't be a problem. A house

is a house and the fact that I've already bought it would be immaterial. I'd hang onto it and then sell it.'

'Life's easy when money's no object.' Alice half-smiled but the eyes that met hers were as remote as ever.

'On the contrary,' Mateo murmured, turning away. 'Money just makes the issues more manageable on a practical level. Everything else remains the same.'

CHAPTER TEN

WHAT THE HECK was going on?

Alice sat in a daze for a while.

She felt as though she'd suddenly been flung onto a rollercoaster and, now that the ride had come to a stop, her head was still all over the place.

Slow anger began to build inside her. Ever since she had skied her way to Mateo's front door in search of help, her easy, predictable, pleasantly normal life seemed to have gone off the rails. Nothing was straightforward any more. And now, having steered herself to some kind of acceptance of what the future would look like, here he went, derailing everything all over again.

While she sat here and stewed, where was he? Back off to his fancy house, where he would probably lose himself in work and put her out of his mind, to be fished out again only when it suited him. Probably when he had to think about supervising the house move.

Was she going to sit around moping, coming to terms with Plan Three Hundred and Three?

No way. She changed her clothes, stuck on something more public-friendly than what she'd shoved on earlier and hunted down a cardigan. Outside, it was a lovely day, blue skies with teasing hints of spring in the air. She decided against public transport and instead called a cab to take her over to Mateo's house.

She'd been there so many times that it no longer impressed her. She'd breathed a sigh of relief that he had never, not once, suggested that she move in with him before the cottage he had bought became available. Maybe he'd known that the soullessness of his house didn't appeal to her on any level.

Or maybe it was a place he saw as his and his alone. It wasn't as if he'd ever intended to get rid of it even once they'd married and were living together in the cottage. He'd said something about its convenience for work purposes, and the added bonus of providing somewhere for clients to stay that wasn't as formal as a hotel if any confidential deals had to be hammered out.

Ha! Had he subconsciously decided to hold on to it because it was back-up for a relationship that might very well fail despite all his upbeat, persuasive chat about it being the ideal solution?

Thoughts occupied her as the taxi made steady progress through the congested streets. She didn't want to go down any rabbit holes or get too absorbed in doubts, questions and uncertainties. She was angry with Mateo for putting her in that place.

She felt a flutter of nerves as the cab came to a stop outside the house. She could see the driver glancing at the impressive property with a certain amount of awe, and she nearly rolled her eyes, because it was such a predictable reaction.

Was it any wonder that the damned man waltzed through life with such overwhelming self-assurance that it was nearly impossible to say *no* to him? Growing up on the wrong side of the tracks had taught him how to be tough and making it to the top of the pile had taught him invincibility. He hadn't got where he had by taking a back seat and being courteous. He'd got where he had by putting himself ahead of the pack and tenaciously making sure he held on to the lead.

The grand house was a spectacle of white, set back from the road and protected from it by wrought-iron gates and an intercom for entry though Alice had a code for the little side gate so there was no need for the intercom. She also had a key to the front door, which she had never used and which she wasn't going to use now. Instead, she rang the doorbell, not even contemplating the fact that Mateo might not be home. Her anger wasn't going to allow that little setback.

She heard the sound of his footsteps and then the door was pulled open and there he was. The flutter of nerves disappeared. She glared at him, hands on her hips, and met his eyes squarely.

'How *dare* you?'

'Come again?' Mateo said, frowning and belatedly stepping aside so that she could sweep past him before spinning round on her heels and resuming her hands-on-hips stance.

'You think you can show up at my leaving do and then get it into your head that because I happened to be *laughing* it was time for you to rethink the whole mar-riage scenario?'

'Can I get you something to drink?'

'I don't want anything to drink, and don't think you can stand there and *prevaricate*. What I do want is for you to tell me why you think you can act like a puppet-master. One minute, there's no marriage; the next minute, you're persuading me that marriage is *the only possible solution* and then, when I've bought into that, getting used to the idea, you decide that you're going to do a U-turn and call the whole thing off!'

'It's not as simple as that.'

Alice followed him as he headed off towards the kitchen, bypassing doors that led to stunningly beauti-ful rooms, most of which were devoid of colour. White walls were interrupted by priceless works of art, and just as priceless rugs were strategically placed on the blonde wooden floors. The whole house soared with space, light, clever windows and arches that made the area seem as vast as a football field, yet there was nothing there that could ever be called *personal*. It was the sanitised space of a billionaire without intimate connections to anyone.

He had a complicated coffee machine which he now started up and it was only after a while, when the cof-fee was poured, that he sat facing her at the metal-and-glass table, long enough to seat ten and about as homey as an ice-pick.

The flutter of nerves returned and Alice knew it was because of the depth of her feelings for him and because of the way his sheer beauty got to her.

'You don't get to do this, Mateo,' she said tightly.

* * *

Mateo raked his fingers through his hair and looked at the plump, sexy woman quietly simmering opposite him. He wanted to scoop her up and carry her off to the bedroom cave-man style, but of course that was the last thing he was going to do. She must have dashed out of the apartment, hot on his heels, because he hadn't been back that long.

'I hope you haven't been using public transport,' he said with a frown, suddenly distracted by the thought of her being jostled on a crowded Tube.

'What does that have to do with anything? And stop changing the subject.'

Mateo lapsed into silence, because this was the last thing he'd been expecting when he'd opened his front door. Yes, he could see why she had stormed over here to find out what was going on, and could see why she felt he'd been pulling her strings and getting her to dance to his tune. What he couldn't understand was why she couldn't see that he was releasing her from an obligation she had never wanted in the first place.

'I'm doing this for you,' he eventually muttered.

'You're doing this *for me.*'

'How many times have you told me that we're not suited? That what you saw in your future was a man who was your soul mate?'

'Things changed when I found out that I was pregnant.'

'Things changed when you saw a picture of me in some trashy magazine with a blonde.'

'Maybe,' Alice admitted uncomfortably.

'Maybe? There's no doubt about it. You thought I'd gone to that function with a woman and I let you believe that because…because I felt that marriage was the best solution. If I got there by exploiting a moment of weakness in you, then all was fair in love and war.'

Mateo flushed darkly and shot her a brooding, challenging gaze.

'What do you mean?'

'I have no idea who that woman was. Someone must have trying to get her mug shot in a magazine. I haven't looked at another woman since…since you.'

'You haven't?'

'Why would I?' He glanced away. He could feel the steady thud of his heart and the racing in his veins as he peered down into an abyss of the unknown.

'Because…'

He heard the faltering in her voice and knew that she was utterly confused. He couldn't blame her, considering he was pretty confused himself: confused by emotions that had overwhelmed him. Confused by an indecisiveness that was so unlike him. Confused as to what to do next.

'I was jealous,' he admitted roughly, and when their eyes met he saw with no great surprise that she was even more bewildered by his impulsive confession. 'I think I've always been jealous when it comes to you and, seeing you there at your leaving party, I wanted you to laugh like that with me. I didn't want you laughing like that with anyone else…but me. I realised that that was something you hadn't done in a while and I knew why.'

He held up one hand although she hadn't interrupted

him. Her mouth was half-open and she was openly gaping. But, now that he had started down the confessional route, Mateo intended to lay his soul bare and complete the journey.

'You'd been coerced into a situation by me. How could you be carefree and light-hearted when you were doing something you didn't really want to do?'

'Don't speak, Mateo. Let *me* do the talking. Honestly, for someone so smart, you can sometimes be so…so… *not smart*. I wasn't light-hearted because I was scared! I was scared that you might see just how much I wanted to marry you! I was so caught up in the effort of trying to hide my feelings for you that it was impossible to be carefree. When you said that I'd wanted more from Simon, you probably didn't know just how right you were. Simon was a shadow, and I know now that any life with him would have been a half-life: a half-life *for me*.

'Mateo, you're the bright light that makes me feel alive! I don't know who I was before I met you, but I wasn't this person—I wasn't this person who felt whole and wonderful and giddy with a thirst to see everything life holds for me, but only with you by my side! I wouldn't have rushed over here like a bat out of hell to find out what the heck was going on if you didn't make me feel the way you do.'

'Alice,' Mateo whispered. 'Everything you've just said…my gorgeous girl…'

'I *want* to marry you, Mateo.'

'And I want to marry *you*, Alice.' He sucked in a shaky breath and met her gaze with steady conviction. 'I want to marry you, and not for the reasons you probably think. Yes, I truly believe that two parents are better than one. Yes, I sincerely think that for the sake of the child we have created it's better for us to be together than apart. And yes, I admit that I was a blind fool, and for far too long didn't look beyond those reasons to unearth the real reason I want to marry you…which is that I love you.'

'You *love me*?'

'You fell through my front door to get out of a blizzard, and in that instant my life changed for ever. I just didn't realise it at the time and, even when it should have been obvious, I ignored it because I'd lived my life assuming that love wasn't something I was capable of feeling. I watched my father disintegrate when my mother died and, even though I loved him, something in me died then and that something was trust in the power of love.

'When Bianca lost the baby we were going to have, I understood how much pain love could bring, because I loved that unborn child. So, Alice, by the time we met I had well and truly built a fortress of steel around my heart, and I was so sure that no one could ever get past it. Yet you proved me wrong. You got past all my barriers as easily as if they had never existed. I just didn't see it at the time.'

'Oh, Mateo.'

Had Alice been expecting this? Not in a million years. Joy flooded her and she leant towards him with bright eyes.

'I've been hiding,' she whispered. 'I fell in love with you after two minutes, and ever since I came round to the idea of marriage I've been hiding my love, protecting my heart, because I thought that if you knew how I felt you'd be appalled.'

'Talk to me. I want to hear.'

'Okay, so, to start with I felt that it would be just too painful being married to you, living with you, loving you and knowing that you were never going to return my feelings. But then when I thought of you with someone else…another woman…'

'A woman I had no idea I was supposedly dating…'

Alice smiled and blushed. 'Well, that's *your* fault for not denying it.'

'Guilty as charged.'

'Well, I knew in a heartbeat that that would be a lot more painful than being with a guy I was crazy about who wasn't crazy about me.'

'So, my darling…' Mateo curved his hand on her cheek and smiled with such tenderness that her heart wanted to burst. 'Now that we've established we need each other and love each other…can I ask for your hand in marriage? A real marriage with love and affection and all the happy-ever-afters I never thought would be on the cards for me. Because I can't live without you.'

'I can't think of anything else in the world…' Alice breathed. 'Anything else on your list of demands? Because, for the record, my answer is *yes*.'

'Now that you mention it…' His voice was low, loving, wickedly sexy.

'Anything.'

'I've discovered that all the money sitting there in my bank account means nothing, because all I want to do is spend it on you, and you've consistently refused to be persuaded into accepting anything from me.'

'Not true!' Alice protested, laughing and delivering tender kisses on his cheek, the side of his mouth and against his neck. 'Okay, largely true.'

'A small church wedding is fine but, before we do that, I want to sweep you off to the Caribbean. Call it a honeymoon before the marriage, because after we're married you might feel just a little too uncomfortable to travel.'

'Well, you've already swept me off my feet, so who am I to object to a little more of the same…?'

Within days, Alice realised that all those signs of opulence—the club where the hush of the fabulously rich had had her gaping, the small but perfectly formed ski chalet, his palatial house in the best postcode in London—all paled in comparison to the black, sleek private jet that flew them to an island in the Caribbean where the wealthy and famous had their discreet, intensely private bolt holes.

From private jet they went on his own small, private yacht to a villa that sat within walking distance from a beach with pale, soft sand that melted into turquoise sea that was calm as a lake. He'd told her to pack light and, so she had, taking the bare minimum, floaty dresses and a hastily purchased maternity swimsuit.

She'd left the tentative warmth of spring to bask in the perfection of tropical heat and enjoyed a week of doing absolutely nothing. She paddled, sat with the warm water lapping around her and watched as Mateo struck out towards a blue horizon, as frighteningly good in the sea as he was on the slopes.

She lay by the side of his infinity pool, shaded by trees with the Technicolor vibrancy of flowering bushes and plants all around, and drowsily listened to the call of birds and the lazy buzz of insects. There was a personal chef who prepared all their food before disappearing at the end of the day, leaving them together to sit on his sprawling veranda with velvety darkness all around them and the sound of the rolling ocean in the background.

And, of course, they made love.

She knew he adored her pregnant body; he explored every inch of it, transporting her to a world of sensory excitement, leaving her sated and complete.

And when after a week they headed back to London, as he helped her into the Range Rover waiting for them at the airfield, he murmured that she was his queen and she could expect a whole lot more of the same in the years to come.

Could anyone have asked for more?

EPILOGUE

MATEO WALKED THROUGH the front door to the sounds of kitchen chaos and smiled. For a few minutes, he stood in the hallway and breathed in the glorious, heady scent of domestic bliss: cooking smells, toddler smells and the aroma of a house lived in, which was so unlike the mansion he had once owned, where everything had felt so sterile in comparison. He'd hung onto that for a couple of months after he and Alice had married, after the most amazing pre-wedding honeymoon a guy could ever have asked for, and had then promptly sold it.

Thoughts of using it if and when he needed to be closer to the office, or if and when he might want to work with a client in privacy, had vanished because, to put it simply, he was quite unwilling to spend a single minute away from his wife if he could help it.

He looked around at the comfortable furnishings: the warm paint on the walls, the clutter of shoes by the door, the tiny yellow wellies with smiley faces, Alice's perpetually mud-splattered green ones and a half-opened umbrella. This was home—the warmth and comfort of family life which he had never envisaged for himself.

He walked towards the sounds of chatter and smiled

from the doorway at just the scene he knew would be waiting for him. Isabella was protesting vehemently at being trapped in a high chair. She was squirming and glaring, her pudgy fingers covered in food, her curly dark hair a cloud around an angry, determined face that was similarly covered in food.

He caught her eye and she stopped, protesting immediately, raising her arms and delivering the sort of beaming smile that got to Mateo every time.

'How do I always know when you're here without having to see you?'

Alice turned to him and her heart swelled with love. They'd been married for two years and the impact he had on her remained the same—had grown, if anything. It wasn't simply because he was just so devastatingly handsome, standing there in a pair of fabulously tailored grey trousers and a white shirt cuffed to the elbows, jacket discarded somewhere between front door and kitchen doorway. No; her heart beat quicker every time, swelled with love and tenderness every time, because when he looked at her it was with such undisguised adoration.

'Tell me,' Mateo drawled, strolling towards his daughter and scooping her up into his arms, regardless of the food that was now going to be deposited on his white shirt or of the little carroty fingers patting his face.

'Whenever Izzy goes silent, I know it's because you've appeared. She knows that she's about to be thoroughly spoiled.'

'If you mean rescuing her from a fate of squished-up vegetables, then I can't deny it.'

He padded towards his wife and looked down at her with adoring eyes, while his daughter did her utmost to get his attention before subsiding against his shoulder with a little gurgle of pure contentment.

'Not that much longer,' he murmured with satisfaction.

'Tell me about it. Was I ever this tired with Izzy?'

Mateo placed his hand protectively on the bump that signalled baby number two. As with Izzy, neither had wanted to find out the sex.

'Probably going to be a boy,' he predicted with a grin. 'Then I can have back-up with you women.'

He pulled her towards him and kissed her as thoroughly as he could with a toddler's head on his shoulder.

'Have I ever told you, my darling, how much I treasure you and how much I thank everything there is to thank that you skied into my life?' He drew back and lovingly stroked her cheek with his thumb. 'I don't know what I'd do without you or this little scrap nodding off on my shoulder. The life I lived before was no life. I've only begun living since I met you.'

'Just what I want to hear,' Alice said approvingly. 'And, now, you'd better go and change before you find your clothes ruined beyond repair with squished up vegetables.'

She reached for their daughter and saw from the flare in her husband's eyes that desire was building in him, a desire she was happy to return.

She grinned. 'And then let's get this evening over

with and have some fun. Because in the blink of an eye we'll be back, my darling, to sleepless nights.'

'I can't wait…'

* * * * *

If you just couldn't get enough of
Snowbound Then Pregnant
then be sure to check out these other dramatic stories
by Cathy Williams!
Unveiled as the Italian's Bride
Bound by Her Baby Revelation
A Wedding Negotiation with Her Boss
Royally Promoted
Emergency Engagement
Available now!